I0691042

A WORKINGMAN'S CEMETERY

© Tim Gooding 2024

All characters in this work are fictitious.
Any resemblance to persons living or dead is purely coincidental.

This book is copyright. Apart from any fair dealing for the purposes of study and research,
criticism, review or as otherwise permitted under the Copyright Act, no part may be repro-
duced by any process without written permission. Inquiries should be made to the publisher.

First published in 2024
Published by Puncher and Wattmann
PO Box 279
Waratah NSW 2298
www.puncherandwattmann.com
web@puncherandwattmann.com

Cover design: Miranda Douglas
Text design and typesetting: Miranda Douglas
Editing: Ed Wright
Printed by Ingram Spark

ISBN 978-1-923099-40-1
A catalogue record for this book
is available from the National Library of Australia.

NATIONAL
LIBRARY OF AUSTRALIA

A WORKINGMAN'S CEMETERY

Tim Gooding

Puncher & Wattmann

to R and EE

CONTENTS

ANGLICAN

ARTHUR FREDERICK PLATT
Born 12 May 1872, Seaham, County Durham
Departed this life 23 August 1945
Loving Husband of Ada, Father of Fred and Jeannie

Arthur Platt, at sixty-nine years of age, possibly more, was the oldest of the stay-in strikers of 1941. Barely able to walk because of his lungs, Arthur was wheeled into the pit, smuggling under his blanket a flask of fortified medicinal *blackjack*. Arthur had no shirt. He wore a holed woollen vest under a buttoned suit coat. Complexion near-blue, he rattled, breathing in short bursts which sounded about to come to a halt. The men remained underground for one hundred and one hours, an industrial record, at which point their demands were met. Fred Platt proudly proclaimed his father also to be one of the strikers who had applied gelignite to the Catherine Hill Bay loading jetty in 1917. Arthur would only admit to knowing the identity of the heroic party.

Durham born and bred, fluent in *Pitmatic*, Arthur resorted to the shaft-dialect of the north east when not wishing to be understood, or in retelling his father's tale of marching four abreast, in black, to the pithead at Pelton Fell, where an explosion of firedamp in the Busty Bank seam, ignited by a miner's safety lamp, had killed twenty four men and boys, including Arthur's grandfather.

Arthur was dusted. "Lungs like concrete", a doctor, unfortunately not the company doctor, had opined. Arthur swore it was *blackjack* – an evil looking, evil smelling fluid, ostensibly herbal, in the main a tincture of licorice and methylated spirits – that kept him alive. His cousin was a veterinary chemist who worked the Wyong track. Arthur sweetened the coal-dark elixir in tea with milk and three sugars.

On his stronger days, Arthur worked the Old Men's Section. Management could not get rid of him. "More seniority than Methuselah," Arthur laughed. When Arthur laughed, comrades held their breath in case it killed him. Heaving, hacking, changing colour, he belted his chest as if something was trying to get out, which never could. Then he spat. What Arthur spat was indescribable. Younger miners topped up his skip when he wasn't looking.

Arthur retired when the aged pension was achieved in 1941. The Old Men's Section quickly disappeared at the same time. Equally quickly the Retired Miners Association was constituted to monitor retired pay and conditions and agitate if necessary. Meetings were held all day every day in a militant corner of the pub. Arthur spent three years in retirement with nothing to do but drink. Beer with a *blackjack* chaser.

His white timber cross having flown north on a southerly, Arthur's grave today is denoted by a brass roundel bearing a number and crowned by a Fowlers Vacola preserving jar hosting a spray of dead flowers. That his barrow has remained stolidly convex under all weathers asserts that Arthur knew what he was doing in requesting interment in clay, not loam. A number of graves occupied by later vintages of miner have become subsidences, after rainfall turning to muddy ponds, crosses protruding, in semblance of the Western Front where a number of neighbours, buried earlier, had served.

Arthur was buried with a goodly supply of *blackjack* in his suitcoat pocket.

STANLEY MORRIS SMITH
b. 30 June 1922 – d. 5 March 1963

Rolling home. Rolling home.

A pair of pigeons, rampant, crown Stan Smith's headstone. Rudely executed in ferro-cement, the precise species to the uneducated eye may appear indeterminate, but to the *fancier* interred below, the memorial avians are, for eternity, Birmingham Rollers.

Rollers had preoccupied Stan since his discovery, at age ten, of a storm-diverted bird roosting overnight on the verandah rail, the refreshed bird in the morning taking to the air and *rolling* homeward. To wit: *backward somersaulting* whilst dropping from the sky as though shot, or perhaps, some theorised, experiencing mid-air *fitting*, at the last instant to pull out of the plunge, ascend to the previous altitude, there under normal circumstances to reunite with feathered colleagues, *the kit*, and continue, in company, *rolling home*. All the way to Birmingham, explained a pigeon fancying neighbour. If a little erratically. *Rolling*, expanded the fancier, led, unfortunately, to tardy, inexact *homing*.

A vision of massed Birminghams *rolling* whilst simultaneously *homing* – promptly and accurately – was to energise Stan's breeding program for a lifetime. A third sub-species, Tumblers, was added to the reproductive mix as Stan experienced a further vision: might the resultant progeny be stimulated simultaneously to *roll*, and *home*, and *tumble*? The performance pigeon trifecta?

There were no women in Stan Smith's life. He would have preferred there were, also, no men. The populous environment of the pit, the proliferation of *talk*, did not sit well with him. How could a man *think*? What was there to talk about, two miles underground, for life? Talk drove him to drink. Alone. Silence spoke acceptably. Ear to the ground, Stan was first to hear of a notably silent, notably solo employment opportunity at the local cemetery. His first task upon securing the position was to bury his predecessor.

Freedom to *think*, to contemplate the world of *Pigeon Digest, Pigeon Record, Pigeon Monthly, Australasian Homing Pigeon*, to wrestle the dialectic of low gravedigger's wages and high pigeon prices, was interrupted by the bombing of Darwin and the unwanted presence of the Japanese in New Guinea. A vision of his Birminghams furnishing the table of hungry Japanese was significant to Stan's enlistment. His anointment of *suspected strike saboteur* Ronald Borthwick as wartime gravedigging locum did not find wide approval among local bereaved.

Returned from hostilities bearing a makeshift mechanical claw (sleeve fashioned from a shell casing) and not wishing to resume his pre-war employment, Stan instead took the TPI pension, built himself a hut in bush on the far side of the lake on the back road to Cessnock, and bred Rollers. Birminghams, with the occasional Galatz or Oriental in the cause of genetic diversity.

Stanley Morris Smith died at forty, having disturbed an Eastern Brown seeking a lunch of fledgling pigeon. Folklore has it that Stan's orbiting somersaulting Rollers shat a memorial circle of guano around the cemetery, the circle of shit growing smaller every day, Stan's grave being the bullseye.

In Loving Memory Of
BRIAN JAMES TRELOAR
3.8.1925 – 1.4.1985
Beloved Son of Elizabeth and Robert
Sadly Missed

Known as Brian to his mother only, some extension of Jimmy 'Skinny' Treloar was forever encased in plaster or makeshift bandage, wired in approximate position, or defying gravity within a foul, ragged sling which doubled as a *snot rag* in addressing the permanent yellow speed stripes on Jimmy's upper lip. 'Chalky-boned', as the affliction was then termed, serial bone fractures, imperfectly repaired, had bequeathed Jimmy a flailing, Cubist walk, propelled by insecurity. None of which rendered the Treloar's only child ineligible to enter the pit at the age of fourteen. In consequence, throughout his strikingly limited schooling, Jimmy sat at the rear of the classroom, gazed out the window, and dreamt expansive schemes of alternative employment, schemes which, not having come to fruition by age fourteen, saw Jimmy's dreaming persist throughout a difficult, injury-plagued time underground, the years of pariahdom consequent upon expulsion from the 1941 Stay-In as a *suspected strike saboteur*, and, finally, deep into enforced semi-retirement on a disability pension supplemented by part-time employ as a bowling club *glassie* and target of solidly militant drinkers' scorn.

Lifelong best mate Ronald Borthwick averred that from very first meeting it was clear that Jimmy Treloar was *a man with a plan*. And, he added, *a clot of the highest order.*

Thus, at the onset of the 1980s, infused with the entrepreneurial spirit of that dawning decade, several *plans* already under his belt, Jimmy came up with what Ronald came to regard as *possibly Jimmy's finest ever get-rich-quick scheme.* Run emus. *Run emus,* Ronald would intone, over and over, in patent awe of his mate's entrepreneurial daring. Within the confines of a tiny company-owned hamlet on the fringe of the northern coalfields, Jimmy was going to *run emus.* Moreover, Jimmy's declared intent was *to run as many of the giant flaming birds as he could fucking lay his bloody hands on.* That the pit was scheduled to close within the year, throwing a final hundred or so fellow villagers out of work, added spice to the *suspected strike saboteur's* business plan.

In the words of Ronald Borthwick:

"Bloody Jimmy had done his research. All the livestock gurus – at least, the ones Jimmy sussed as in total agreement with the Treloar Economic Outlook – reckoned there wasn't a single part of the emu that humans couldn't use. Eyeballs. Toenails. Arsehole. Feathers. Everything. The whole fucking emu. His second-latest plan – monopolising the local Outdoor Home Improvement market once the pit had closed and the village gentrified – was suddenly right out the window. Jimmy was getting himself a herd of emus. Herd? A mob. Running the birds where they used to run the pit ponies was my idea. Fix the fences first, I told him. Emus love to kick down fences. Hand it to Jimmy, he was way ahead of me. He'd figured out a way he wouldn't need fences at all. He was going to brand the emus and free range them. He never specified exactly where on the emu body he was going to apply the J.T. brand. In the event that branding the emus was not a goer, Jimmy was going to tag the birds. Somewhere. Emus don't have ears, but there'd be somewhere. Wait, there's more. Free Range Emu was only part one of his plan, which was a work of genius, even if he did say so himself,

9

but part two was even more genius. You know what he was going to feed J. Treloar Premium Grade Free Range Emus? Agapanthus. Agafuckingpanthus! Those flowers like purple and white toilet brushes you see all over the place now. South African. Like Bitou Bush. And Cape Daisy. Jimmy reckoned emus and agapanthus were a natural fit and it was only a fucking miracle no-one had thought of it before. He had a point. Agapanthus were growing like topsy everywhere. Out front of every home. Up every suburban driveway. Wild in the bush. Throughout the National Parks. On top of Uluru. Everywhere. Jimmy planned to free range his emus in and around the village to fatten them up, then muster and drove the birds to market, tucking into agapanthus – with a side salad of bitou bush and cape daisy – if only emus ate lantana! – all the way to the killing floor. He was serious. You just wanted to punch him. He'd lost his marbles. He wasn't the only one. In 1981 they gave him one of those credit cards.

He had me fooled too. It was the chalky bones."

Jimmy Treloar lies in Anglican, Ronald Borthwick a distance away, in Presbyterian. The casual visitor is unlikely to notice that the pair share an identical date of decease.

In Fond Remembrance Of
ROBERT WILLIAM TRELOAR
12 December 1903 – 1 January 1929
Beloved husband of Betty, father of Brian
Drowned in The Entrance Channel

ELIZABETH ANN TRELOAR
b. 3 October 1906   d.15 April 1989
Beloved wife of Robert, mother of Brian

Bob and Betty Treloar rest side by side beneath a featureless concrete slab more king single than double, their cramped proximity an unintended consequence of Betty's longevity, delayed excavation of her allocation allowing for territorial encroachment of *a good foot and a half*, in the measurement of the time, by a neighbouring grave occupied by Percival Fleetwood Frost. Having miscalculated under the influence of Red Mill OP Rum, noting the error in a more sober light, incumbent *bone orchardist* Ronald Borthwick dismissed remediation by concluding that once a hole is dug, it stays dug.

It was whispered by certain parties that Bob Treloar bore the blood of both invader and invaded, in long forgotten ratio, although it was thought probable the blood of the invaded had mingled with that of invader early in the piece. What led to the whispers was unclear. Perhaps it was simply that Bob had darkish skin and what was attributed a freakish sixth sense when playing football. Bob himself was only dimly aware of some possible happenstance 'back then', but what had

11

happened, if it had happened, he chose not to explore. The presence of convict or aboriginal blood on a branch of the family tree did not, at the time, excite investigation.

Solidarity was everything in the pit. The Australian Coal and Shale Employees' Federation, on the cutting edge of industrial agitation, embraced communism, socialism, anarcho-syndicalism, and any number of associated left sectarian tendencies and splinter groups, all of whose manifestos promoted racial equality. Theory and practice found frequently not to be in alignment, Bob Treloar kept himself to himself and trod lightly the traditional path of underground advancement from trapper boy to clipper to wheeler to hewer of coal, before meeting his untimely demise.

As the year 1928 came to a close, Bob caught fire on New Year's Eve in The Entrance, and either burnt to death or drowned in the channel trying to put himself out. Enacting a traditional New Years Eve ritual, Bob and several other parties were endeavouring to raze the wooden bridge connecting the southern half of the town with its cross-channel twin. Alertness of police and fire brigade had thwarted numerous annual attempts to burn the structure to the waterline. For no seeming reason other than it was there. And constructed of timber. On the New Year's Eve of Bob's death, however, an uncontained bushfire sparked by a tourist's cigarette had torn across the western ridge to threaten the fringe of several coastal towns, and concentrate the minds of local services. In consequence, while a red glow outlined hills on the inland horizon, closer to the coast flames leapt at several points from The Entrance channel bridge. Success finally tasted, festive exuberance led Bob Treloar to a celebratory dance in Christmas pyjamas that proved inflammable. The channel was running hard on a king tide.

Elizabeth Ann Treloar, née Appleton, of Anglo-Saxon mining stock, was reared to be a coal-winner's wife, so to embrace misadventure – lay-offs and cavils out, strikes, sickly children, injury, sudden death – as a permanent feature of life. The duty of the miner's wife was to be prepared. If not prepared, to make do. Two weeks prior to her husband's decease, Betty had persuaded Bob Treloar to invest in a dairy cow obtained cheaply from a new friend. Betty had also planted a vegetable garden using seed procured at no cost from the same unidentified friend, and similarly sourced three chickens. Bob fox-proofed the chicken house and, at Betty's insistence, covertly drowned a neighbour's cat. That a home-grown diet had no beneficial effect upon the chalky bones of son Jimmy perturbed his mother, the perturbance worsening as Jimmy elected to displace meagre dining with smoking like a chimney and drinking like a fish.

Bob's fiery but wet demise having preceded the onset of The Great Depression by a matter of months, Betty took in the washing and ironing and cleaned the offices and residences of several echelons of mine management, duties resulting in an encounter with mine under-manager Willy Goldfinch, in the wake of which Betty continued discreetly to encounter Willy on mutually convenient occasions. For his part, Willy looked kindly upon fatherless Jimmy and, when opportunity arose, secured his transitory de facto stepson work 'up top' as a token-collecting boy and billy boiler, occupations less challenging to brittle bones and fear of the dark than labour underground. Following soon upon Jimmy's expulsion from the pit during the 1941 Stay-In, the gift of a new lawnmower facilitated the boy's move to an alternative career. *Certain people* – unkind people, thought Betty – opined that the mower was reward from mine management for services rendered. Betty knew otherwise, having been assured both by her son and under-manager Goldfinch that Ronald Borthwick was the party responsible for smuggling beer into the stay-in and resultant adverse coverage in conservative newspapers, Jimmy simply an unwitting dupe to his best mate's assault on strike credibility.

It was said that Betty had *an eye*. Much as, prior to Bob's death, she had made the acquaintance of a man with a cow, seed and three chickens, Betty continued to make the acquaintance of helpful friends in the wake of her abandonment by Willy Goldfinch. Discount replacement blades from a Belmont hardware merchant facilitated Jimmy's continued pursuit of a lawnmowing empire. On the infrequent occasions when pork found its way onto the Treloar table via an acquaintance in an abattoir or the befriending of a wild pig shooter passing through, Betty, also knowing a man who knew an applegrower, could always accompany the pig with apple sauce. A further close friend gifted Betty a leaky boat, deployed by Jimmy and Ronald in crabbing by night on Lake Macquarie, until the vessel sank. Additional benefit accrued from familiarity with a man in the liquor trade. Determined that she and son would never go without, from time to time Betty also worked nights in Swansea.

PERCIVAL FLEETWOOD FROST
b. 5 June 1906 – d. 27 August 1958
Beloved Son of Elizabeth and Robert
Take The Odds

The final resting place of Perce Frost, at the intersection of Anglican and Roman Catholic Lanes, while not the equal of a pyramid of Egypt, remains an imposing edifice, which of all domiciles in the cemetery appears most likely to deter tomb robbers. A massive slab of pink granite, sparkling quartz, surmounted by polished black marble featuring Gothic inscription in gold, the assemblage constitutes a sepulchre befitting the bones of an SP bookie acquainted with several trainers and jockeys and sadly missed by a large family.

Swept-back hair glowing Californian Poppy gold, Perce wheezed, coughed, and spat his odds. Perce had been medically assessed as twenty-five percent dusted, for which he could derive twenty five per cent compensation. Deeming the figure insufficient, Perce opted to remain underground and in consequence lose an arm to a falling floater in E Section. The pony hauling the chain cutter panicked and snapped a hind leg. Shot and snigged to the surface, the animal's destination thereafter became the subject of rumour. Duly elected checkweighman pursuant to this misfortune, the position a convenient crossroads for punter and bookie alike, Perce stored turnover within his folded coat sleeve and counted cash and wrote tickets one-handed. He wheezed sympathy to requests for credit, his clients being neighbours and workmates, all of whom, despite straitened circumstances, considered welching worse than murder.

The Stay-In of 1941 saw Perce finger Johnno Jones, still in the pyjama shorts and singlet worn when dragged drunk out of bed, as the mongrel who had rendered Perce's daughter Nell 'up the duff'. Mid-industrial action over safety issues linked to mechanisation[1] , Perce and several mates with both arms convinced Black Sheep Jones Boy Johnno to do the right thing by Nell upon completion of the Stay-In, whereupon Johnno Jones became, overnight, superbly militant and determined to Stay In as long as humanly possible. Nell gave birth to a baby girl, Janice, the day after Johnno's secret enlistment in the army. Johnno was blown to bits by a grenade in Borneo. The baby grew up to be 'Moaning' Janice Jones. When her time came, Moaning Janice's ashes were scattered seaward from atop Nobby's Head.

Late career Perce Frost encountered stiff competition for SP custom in the swarthy, black-curly-haired form of George the Greek. George operated a barber's shop in Belmont. Miners had their hair cut on Saturday mornings. Saturday was also race-day. In the end, Perce could not compete. By then, it mattered little, Perce finding himself a great deal more than twenty-five per cent dusted. Perce had worked for a time at Metropolitan on the southern field, where twenty-five per cent was called *a good start*. The assessing quack was management-appointed, not to mention a Pom.

It was loudly and frequently acknowledged in Retired Miners Corner that Perce Frost, had he not died of the dust, would have *fucking detested* local dishlicker 'Mystery Man', owner and trainer Andy Gemmell, for the crime of inexplicably successful performances, at outlandish odds, on the nearby Wyong dog track. 'Mystery Man' disappeared in mysterious circumstances. His weighted remains were discovered at the bottom of a backyard well following a drought.

---

[1]Rushed post-war mechanisation was accompanied by mechanisation of injury. New machines were not designed to fit old shafts. Roof timbering was knocked down. Power cutters and perforators produced more, and finer dust, than previously

SARAH MAY BORTHWICK
3.3.1904 – 15.8.1957
Wife Of Malcolm
Mother Of Dorothy and Ronald
Grandmother of Shelley
Shadows we are. Shadows we pursue

Sarah May Borthwick, née Butcher, was conceived aboard the mail ship S.S. Ormuz en route to Australia as, in an uncommon demonstration of co-operation by the elements, the vessel traversed a calm section of ocean. So would claim her father, Harry, out of earshot of her mother, Elaine. As to how the conception was managed in steerage, Pop Butcher did not go into detail. Sarah was born and raised in 'Geordieland', an enclave of Tynesiders recruited to the southern hemisphere by a fellow Northumberlander, a manager in charge of hiring and firing, who liked to know what he was getting, and when the time came, getting rid of. Neither of Sarah's parents were Geordies. Their daughter nevertheless acquired an accent she found hard to shake off.

Sarah accepted that the chances were she would become a coalminer's wife, yet was intent on becoming one as far away from her mother as possible. Sarah hated fuss. Her mother vibrated with it. Aware that fuss may serve to fill a marital vacuum, Sarah forgave Elaine. Forgiveness turned to screaming after an hour in the same room. Her mother's reaction was incomprehension, followed by affront, followed by guilt, all of which, after shows of penitence by her daughter, proceeded into storage.

At eighteen, in Kurri Kurri, attending a dance to raise funds for miners gone out in the 'Major Crane'[2] strikes, the opportunity to bolt from fuss presented in the shape of flame-haired miner Malcolm Borthwick. Escape was not to be complete. The presence of maternal fuss at the wedding, at the births of Dorothy and Ronald, and throughout subsequent commemorative occasions, was unavoidable. Ronald's extravagantly delayed entry into the world was attributed, in private and not completely in jest, to the grandmother's hovering presence in an apparently shrinking house having stimulated the mother's insides to clench, and the baby wilfully to resist emergence. When the child finally began to budge on the evening of the twenty-first, Sarah felt that she and her impending offspring had reached an accord. The sooner the fuss returned to Geordieland, the better. Expanding in later life upon his protracted birthing, Ronald would claim that he clung on within *"like a cat on a carpet"* because he knew what was coming.

Malcolm vanished without explanation after twelve years of marriage. Putative widow Sarah thereafter made do with handouts, fish, rabbit, the vegetable garden which responded positively to Malcolm's absence, and local credit, before obtaining intermittent employment in the Kurri Kurri miners co-op.

She resolutely undertook the hour-and-a-half walk to and from work for two years before being gifted an unused bicycle by widower 'Short' Owen Jones. Short Owen went on to gift dressed rabbits, a brace of traps, and young Ronald Borthwick the advance to buy the second-hand shotgun, which was to feature prominently in his later life, before Sarah consented to be escorted to a showing, in Newcastle, of *The Wizard Of Oz*.

[2]Major Crane. Magistrate notorious for ruthless gaoling of striking miners under the Masters And Servants Act.

Seven years of popular movies later, Malcolm legally deceased, Short Owen saw fit to propose. Sarah, answering in the affirmative, proceeded to identify serial reasons to delay: wartime circumstances, rationing and the like, underlain by fear, hope, or both, that dead Malcolm might yet turn up. The declaration of peace saw Sarah run out of excuses. Short Owen proved himself a dark horse, revealing the accumulation of funds, not necessarily with complete legality, for an extended honeymoon in Wales.

Sarah detested Wales, the cold, the wet, the relatives and by the end, Short Owen. More than ever, she found her body inhabited by the spirit of her mother. The shuddering away of fuss, the stiffening of inner defences, distraction, no longer sufficed to banish the presence.

Sailing the same route as that upon which her life had begun, Sarah developed pneumonia and died shortly after entering Sydney heads. At night, ear to the slab, claims daughter Dorothy, Gramma Borthwick can be heard saying *"I told you so"*, over and over.

An angled block of speckled stone at the head of Sarah's grave bears the quotation: "Shadows we are. Shadows we pursue." The nature of Sarah's relation to Edmund Burke remains unknown.

SAMUEL MALCOLM BORTHWICK
b. 30 July 1901 –
Husband Of Sarah
Father Of Dorothy and Ronald
He Loved To Fish

Malcolm Borthwick's grave, reserved in 1934, in Presbyterian, relocated in 1942, to Anglican, remains to this day unoccupied and marked by a headstone lacking in finality.

Malcolm was christened Samuel Malcolm in memory of Samuel Horne, drowned at age ten, along with a further twenty-five child workers, in the Huskar colliery disaster of 1838. Malcolm's grandmother had insisted upon the industrial importance of her childhood playmate's continued commemoration. Her grandson's submergence in a fontful of cold transported Calvinism, as an echo of his namesake's fate, went unnoticed. Malcolm seized the opportunity to dispense with the unwanted label upon enrolling himself on the first day of school.

Malcom's father Charlie died beneath a runaway skip in 1911, his legacy red hair, rubbery crescent smile, dark suit, boots, shovel, pick, mandrills, pinch bar, hatchet, borer, drills, bits, powder tin, crib tin, and water bottle. Weekly, as a boy, Malcolm would lay out the collection upon his share of bedroom floor to ponder their meaning, before cleaning and oiling the metal, rubbing dripping into the leather, in anticipation of progress into the pit upon turning fourteen.

In 1917, then a pit wheeler, he joined striking men lining a clifftop to pelt with rocks scab labour arriving from Sydney, as women kettled the blacklegs with metal pots and spoons. Baton-wielding police pursued the strikers through the town. Malcolm took refuge under the house, in the company of border collie Rowdy, who deemed proceedings a great game until joined by an unnamed Germanic police dog. The police broke three of Malcolm's ribs expressing disappointment that a gelignite box discovered under his bed contained only an old suit and newspaper obituary dating from 1911.

Malcolm's graduation from wheeler to coalface hewer came amid loudening whispers of the role's extinction, as the spectre of mechanisation stalked the pits with post-war vigour. Early model cutters, electric chains and windy picks, were already deployed in the old section. Despite promises, men had been laid off. There had been accidents. Machines were noisy. Miners needed to hear the roof talk.

On his back in an undercut, hewing with pick or hatchet, one handed, there was almost daily a moment when Malcolm became piquantly aware of the weight of the world inches above his face, and considered that it could render him as flat as a stamp before he knew it. 'Bottom-holing' was deemed the most dangerous activity of all in winning coal the old way. It would be simple to kick out the supports, he thought. Slam. Gone. Publicly he projected a rubbery smiling nonchalance. He rarely spoke when not spoken to. The Pit considered Malcolm's an open face, painted on a closed door.

Miners wanted sons. So it went. The tradition wove as a black ribbon back to the old, dark, cold country. Yet Malcolm felt relief upon learning his first child was a daughter. And that Dot's hair was a light, mousey brown. He accepted as fate, the later arrival of violently red-haired son Ronald.

In his mother's eyes, Malcolm "were soft". He lacked gravitas. His claiming to have coined the term 'rationalisation' upon finding

21

conventional terminology inadequate to encompass the golden future of coalmining, and similar political levities, failed to wring amusement from Gramma. Yet he attended the pit when the whistle blew, went on the coal 'deficient' or not, was solid in dispute, resisted 'speed up', struck against the dangers of mechanical pillar extraction, like every other good man. When the whistle failed to blow, he trapped rabbits, caught fish, oversaw a dying garden. He married a woman he loved. Fathered two children. Played team sport. Drank black with a Red Mill chaser. Spat dark phlegm. None of which indicated softness. But yet again, he *was* soft. It was in his smile. Gramma never realised that Malcolm smiled when disappointed.

He fished to unwind. An activity solitary and above ground, the loading jetty at Catherine Hill Bay his favourite spot, favourite time Saturday night, on a rising tide and no moon. No work next day, nothing overhead but stars. On a still night the noise from the pub reached the end of the jetty. A thousand feet out to sea, legs dangling above the high-water mark, flask of Red Mill at hand, rolling a cigarette inside his coat, he could, he felt, cast his line over the edge of the world.

He vanished while fishing. A body was not found. The Pit entertained suspicions. Sightings of wiry red-haired men thought to resemble missing person Malcolm Borthwick were made up and down the east coast of New South Wales and southern Queensland, mostly during holiday periods. Malcolm, or someone not unlike him, was observed drinking to excess in hotels at Ulladulla, Bulahdelah, Brunswick Heads, and Mooloolaba. He was reported drinking and fishing from the breakwater at Iluka, off the bridge at The Entrance, the rocks at Avoca Beach, and piers at Long Jetty and Greenwell Point. Journeying by bus to a miner's wedding in Helensburgh, near Wollongong, Betty Treloar claimed to have espied Malcolm hitch-hiking outside the Kangy Angy roadhouse, where, before Betty could intercept him, he accepted a lift in a grey Austin with Queensland number plates and garish black and gold fringed souvenir cushions on the back seat, driven by a young woman who, according to Betty Treloar, looked *fast*. War declared, Malcolm was reported boarding a troopship bound for the United Kingdom. Twenty five years after the disappearance, seeking a parking spot on the Gold Coast, Cedric Keats motored past a red-bearded but otherwise balding man, beach rod in one hand, fingers of the other up the gills of a huge flathead, having his photograph taken in front of a 'Single Men Only' boarding house in Coolangatta. The man was gone by the time Cedric had parked his car, boat, and home-made caravan. The boarding house disclaimed knowledge of a red bearded lodger. No photograph of fisherman and flathead ever turned up. The notice in the corner store window quickly aged in the Gold Coast sun.

ELAINE VICTORIA BUTCHER
20 October 1890 –12 November 1959
Beloved Wife of Harry
Mother of Sarah
Grandmother of Dorothy and Ronald
Great Grandmother of Shelley
In His Garden

HAROLD FRANCIS BUTCHER
4 August 1883 – 16 May 1961
Beloved Husband of Elaine
Father of Sarah
Grandfather of Dorothy and Ronald
Great Grandfather of Shelley
Reunited

Harry 'Pop' Butcher sported a mediaeval-esque leather helmet with a single shoulder flap as after midnight he ferried cans to and from backyard dunnies in the coalfields. He enjoyed the work. The night air. The exercise. The solitude. *The slopping shit.* In the face of *the creeping menace of septic tanks and sewerage,* he remained confident the smaller, more isolated pit towns and their primitive facilities would last just long enough to see him through to the end. Referring to his cart, Pop was heard to say, more than once, "It'd be a humdinger if it had a bell on it." Pop possessed a number of favourite sayings with a tendency to emerge irrespective of relevance.

Returned post-siege from Ladysmith, ex-soldier Harry found the pits and docks of Bristol, the Wills tobacco factory production line, Somerset itself, of limited interest. Australia beckoned. He had encountered Australians in South Africa, appreciated their crudeness and apparent freedom. Sea passage booked, returning to Bristol by train, he encountered Elaine Hammond, of Bath. A draper's daughter seemingly above his station, urgent courting was to Harry's surprise promoted with enthusiasm by the intended's father. The couple married three days in advance of Harry's Australian ticket becoming void.

Fellow West Country refugees found to be scarce in the Hunter coalfields, after prolonged wandering having rented a tiny abode in the node of North Easterners that was 'Geordieland', Elaine set about establishing a landlocked island resembling a country cottage in Somerset. Rapprochement between English country garden and Australian conditions was to prove a lifelong challenge. Flowers made Elaine Butcher happy. That the robust adventurousness she admired in her spouse would culminate in the role of night soil collector to a cluster of tiny pit towns in Australia, Elaine could not have foretold. Nor predicted Harry more specifically collecting the nightsoil of an unlikely union of daughter Sarah and coal miner Malcolm, in a begrimed village known to longtime locals, not without affection, as The Pit.

In later years, Elaine would appear through the working week to dress as for Sunday church, in midwinter, in Somerset. Her youthful prettiness became vase-like. Cracks appeared. She began to fuss. Fuss, with remnant Somerset accent, became the embroidery of life, adding colour and line to diminished circumstances. Fuss cost nothing, could be manufactured out of nothing, was applicable to everything and available to everybody, no matter how humble. Fuss was both every-day and ceremonial, equally irradiating births, deaths, cups of tea and what to wear. To fuss was to love. Love, outside St Mary's, Weston, came close to ruining daughter Sarah's wedding. Later family gatherings, similarly infused with love, were similarly rendered fraught.

Pop smiled and didn't care. He believed he had married up, worshipped accordingly, had no ambition beyond providing for his beloved and their daughter. When another war called, a night before moving up, he claimed to have bumped into Field Marshall Douglas Haig, well to the rear of a battlefield located in a foul bog known as Wipers. *"Don't be vague. Blame General Haig."* War taught that anything could happen at any time. Blameworthy Generals became Field Marshalls. He declined to march on Anzac Day, in later years watched the celebrations on television.

The coalfields dunnyman was union solid in dispute, steadfastly refusing, whenever duty called, to collect the shit of *scabs*. Famously, the Rothbury lockout of 1929 having dragged on into 1930 and a summer heatwave, dysentery, stench, blowflies and engorged mosquitoes added zest to Pop's already pungent militancy. The buzzing, the *hum*, became noxious well in advance of the scab camp.

A letter to say that her father had killed himself saw Elaine conclude that, in encouraging union with Harry and travel to the far side of the world, he had simply wanted to clear the decks first. That she was not in Bath to save him with love added impetus to the journey from fuss to nervous collapse. The predecease of daughter Sarah informed Nan's complete breakdown.

Gone missing, located shuffling up and down the aisle of a citybound train, swearing at anyone who dared look at her, Nan Butcher had never before, in her entire life, been heard to swear. Nor was her cursing from the mild end of the spectrum. Nan's mouth became foul, f*** and c***, you f****** c***, much in the vein of pit men when something went truly, dangerously haywire. Where she had encountered such language was a mystery. She swore at Pop as well, called him a f****** c***!, cursed him as The Devil. When he took her flowers or chocolates she would hurl them back screaming "Get thee behind me, Satan, you f****** c***!" He visited her in the safe unit every day.

Electro-convulsive therapy in the wake of a second breakdown reduced but did not eliminate Nan's affliction. Her profanity seemed to quieten, appear more resigned.

Harry, with great affection, would recall that Elaine's last words to him were a trembling whisper, "You little shit."

Aware that heaven presented as an infinite flower garden, eternally scented, forever in bloom, Harry capped his beloved's resting place with an expansive collection of unalike vases within which, weekly, he would place fresh flowers.

Pop endured eighteen months without Elaine before being found on the kitchen floor by a local widow, she persistent in the face of Pop's express disinterest in just happening to be passing by with cooked meals.

Ronald Borthwick buried his grandparents alongside his mother Sarah. Despite an inkling that Elaine might well deem their double-depth grave improper and become restless, Pop Baker considered vertical reunion well worth taking the chance. Matching family headstones were commissioned and purchased by Ronald's sister, Dorothy. She, a smoker, could save. He, a drinker, could not.

PRESBYTERIAN

GEOFFREY WILFRED CLUTTEN
1896 – 11 July 1943
RIP Tinsnips

Shortly after arrival behind the lines, 'Tinsnips' Clutten was kicked in the head by a Belgian or possibly French horse while attempting to stretch a Belgian or possibly French chicken's neck in a bomb-blasted barn somewhere south west of Polygon Wood, the powers-that-be thus finding the excuse they had been seeking to ship Tinsnips home and back into the pit. As a coalminer, his enlistment had been officially resisted in the first place but Tinsnips had put his foot down.

Back underground, metal plate holding cracked skull together, shirtless above grimy shorts and hobnailed boots, Tinsnips seemed never to stop smiling. Co-workers could not decide whether his faculties had been diminished by the horse's hoof or that the permanent smile merely indicated adoption of a simpler attitude to life. The injury did not seem to affect his ability to play the cornet – the only time he stopped smiling – and he remained a stalwart of The Pit Brass Band.

Malcolm Borthwick crowned returned serviceman Tinsnips the fastest wheeler in the pit, the award a mixed blessing: "Tinsnips never bloody stops!" Towards the end Malcolm was heartily sick of Tinsnips and his haste. "Too many bloody *you'll do's*", he would say, searching pockets. At week's end, a good wheeler might receive a "you'll do" – a small amount of cash – as reward for service

The roof collapse was small by historic standards. Water did not gush from above, tunnels were not flooded. Rock had likely been loosened by an earlier goaf collapse. Only Tinsnips' head and shoulders were visible. Co-workers dug him out with bare hands. Eleanor Morgan galloped Moonlight through thick bush to fetch the doctor from Swansea.

Tinsnips was a bachelor – he had a mother somewhere, no-one could remember where – and resided in a shanty which sagged in the middle, as though painted on canvas draped over a drooping rope. Inside, flooring dipped where the ground beneath had subsided into an abandoned working. Rent for the patchwork of timber, iron and hessian bagging was deducted from Tinsnips' fortnightly pay packet. Towers of newspapers and beer bottles restricted entry via the front door. His colleagues lay him on the foul single bed and left. He lingered for nine months.

The Pit Brass Band led the funeral procession. Miners in hats and dark suits marched two abreast behind the coffin, the box proceeding precariously due to Short Owen Jones' lack of height. Trailing women wore hats or subdued hair with scarves. Tinsnips' mother had not been found. The column crossed the white bridge and wound its way to the Presbyterian section which, Tinsnips' persuasion being unknown, was considered a reasonable guess and convenient. The band completed 'The Dead March', Minister Sefton spoke of the promise of the life hereafter, Short Owen Jones sang a beautiful 'Bread Of Heaven'. Remnants of jam tarts and a beer bottle on the grave floor were not remarked upon. The band played with less rigour as mourners wandered back up the hill, beyond which lay the pub. The women went home. Gravedigger Ronald Borthwick hand-painted relevant details on the wooden cross. 1896 as the year of Tinsnips' birth was also considered a reasonable guess.

MERVYN DAVID FERRIS

b. 12 November 1897 – d. 25 February 1974

Beloved husband of Olwen and Sian

Devoted Father of Nerys

Grandfather of Dimity

Mervyn Ferris came through Gallipoli and the Western Front unscathed until June 1917 when, prior to the Battle Of Messines Ridge, he was caught under a gas shell barrage in Ploegsteert (Plugstreet) Wood. Unable to take part in the ensuing Third Battle Of Ypres, later more commonly known as Passchendaele, Mervyn was to conclude that, although sleeping with an oxygen tank by the bed for the remainder of his life was an inconvenience, his gassing had been a fortunate occurrence.

Invalided to a hospice in south London, Mervyn found himself closely attended by nurse Olwen Matthews, an interest in the Australian and his homeland stemming from her family having been caught on Southampton docks, mid-emigration southward, by the outbreak of war. Mervyn and Olwen married the following year, only for Olwen to die six months later, of Spanish flu, as did their unborn child.

Damaged lungs discouraging work underground, Mervyn was offered employment on the screens, later in the washery. Locked out in 1929, baton-clubbed and savaged by a police dog at Rothbury, ex-AIF Sergeant Ferris joined more than four hundred war veteran miners presenting honourable discharge papers at a door in Kurri Kurri and enlisting in the newborn Labor Defence Army. Drilling on Kurri Kurri football ground, the assemblies were mocked by monitoring police for the absence of armaments and antique Great War drill procedures. In response, at training's end the units would loudly repeat the chant heard at Rothbury: "Guns. Guns. Give us guns!" The government and enforcement services took pains to ensure as few guns as possible fell into their hands.

Some guns there were, however. Mervyn had been gifted a .22 rifle on his fifteenth birthday. At Ashtonfields, police diverted elsewhere by a ruse, Mervyn and variously-armed fellow veterans covered civilian miners engaged in alerting scabs to the error of their ways, torching sulkies, driving off horses, and harrying *blacklegs* stripped naked through the surrounding scrub.

In the aftermath of Ashtonfields, *Basher Gangs*, embracing the most marginal interpretations of the Unlawful Assemblies Act, attended to any gathering larger than the legal three, finally, en masse to sweep the South Maitland coalfield – Kearsley, Abermain, Kurri Kurri – in waves charging popular assemblies, clubbing and trampling under horses' hooves men, women and children.

A subsequent defensive patrol along the main street of Cessnock led Mervyn to witness the ghost of his wife Olwen in the doorway of the co-op. The apparition revealed herself to be Olwen's younger sister, Sian. The Matthews family, upon cessation of hostilities, had made it off the Southampton docks. Unable to live up to the memory of her sister, Sian departed not long after giving birth to a daughter, Nerys.

In later life, Mervyn sought solace in the embrace of The Queen Of The Nile, the bowling club poker machine. Cleopatra remained well ahead, begrudgingly coughing up small change only. Subscribing to talk of a management fix, which seemed also to afflict the cigarette machine and public phone, Mervyn found himself ripping down

Cleo's arm in mounting disquiet before the heart attack.

He died as the first oil shock saw a recovery in the prospects of coal, which like previous industrial recoveries, was not to last.

Mervyn is commemorated in mid-grey granite, the original slab of which, recalled stonemason Vincent 'Jumpy' Bates, fell with several others off the back of a truck en route to cladding a bank building in western Sydney. A posthumous embrace of Presbyterianism by the avowed atheist Mervyn was facilitated by gravedigger Ronald Borthwick, acting under instruction from the deceased's daughter. Nerys Ferris claimed to be unimpressed by the sandy soil and prospects of long-term security within the Non-Denominational/Other sector, her father's original destination.

Dedicated To The Memory Of
NERYS DAWN FERRIS
Born 23 November 1926
Called Home 14 August 2017
A Tower Of Strength

It was said the sneer of Nerys Ferris could boil a billy. It was said her hair shone on a dark day and she knew it. It was said she would come to a sticky end. Known from cradle onward *to have bigger fish to fry*, the less diplomatic tagged The Queen Of The Pit *a shandy pisser*. That at seventeen, possibly sixteen, Nerys Ferris would attract the attention of mine undermanager Willy Goldfinch, finesse the sacking of his secretary so as to take her position, oust widow Betty Treloar as Willy's bit on the side, see off Willy's wife Adrienne to parts and fate unknown, move up, socially and geographically, into the Goldfinch residence atop Snob Hill, there speedily to produce a daughter, ostensibly to Willy, surprised no-one except the earlier Goldfinch children. That when Willy entertained important visitors his teenage *amour* ate in the kitchen, alone, also failed to surprise.

Nerys Ferris's Welsh Presbyterianism, Willy Goldfinch's Germanic Methodism both being found unable to compete with Gothic Revival Anglican, daughter Dimity Dilys Ferris-Goldfinch was christened in Christ Church Cathedral, Newcastle, the showiest house of worship in the region. Below Snob Hill it was noted that Dimity did not in any way resemble Willy Goldfinch. Whom she did resemble varied according to taste. Ronald Borthwick did not rate a mention.

Nerys Ferris had claimed, from schooldays onward, to be the love of Ronald Borthwick's life, a notion with which he was in befuddled agreement. Ronald's prospects, however, never came within coo-ee of making the Nerys Ferris grade, which stipulated mine management, brick house included in salary package, as a minimum. Nerys Ferris would nevertheless derive lifelong utility from her cultivation of Ronald's ardour, cognisant of the fact that, as long as the ardour remained unreciprocated, strategic deployment of a particular gap-toothed smile, exposure of a strawberry-freckled shoulder, could always convince Ronald he was definitely in with a chance if he were only to do her this one special little favour. In their shared school years, her encouragement of his affection would peak on April Fools Day: "Will you be my boyfriend, Ronald? Would you like to see my undies, Ronald? Meet me behind the slack heap. I'll show you my growler. April Fool."

Ronald duly responded to such displays of affection in kind. On 1 April 1940 the *Newcastle Herald* carried an item concerning "a well-endowed young female scantily clad in rabbit fur" sighted running through bushland near Mooney Mooney. Picking up the item, the Sydney-based *Daily Telegraph* dubbed her the "Mooney Mooney Nymph". Nerys Ferris was not flattered by certain aspects of the nymph's physical description to the degree envisaged by beau Ronald Borthwick.

The reign of Nerys Ferris atop Snob Hill lasted a bare six months. If nothing else, The Queen Of The Pit's teak vocal chords and ballistic upward inflection returned Willy Goldfinch to the spidery arms of his wife.

By closure of the pit, every miner whom Nerys Ferris had found not important enough to step out with, was dead. Mine management was gone. The fly-in fly-out administrators, Nerys Ferris quickly discovered, were cold fish. Reluctantly she was compelled to take up with Bowling Club Manager Alan Goodge, divorcee, retired suburban solicitor, recent village blow-in, until the sober gentleman's bicycling accident, following which Nerys Ferris foreclosed on the opposite sex. The death of Jimmy 'Skinny' Treloar saw Nerys Ferris elect not to attend the funeral, an event even more uncrowded than the lowering of Ronald Borthwick, this occurrence an hour earlier, which Nerys Ferris did see fit to attend, loudly. Nerys Ferris had been wise to Skinny Treloar all along. Ronald Borthwick, her dupe in other matters, had refused to believe her until the last.

Nerys Ferris duly instructed the gathering of Dot Borthwick, Cedric Keats, and Minister Sefton, pointing into the grave:

"I warned him. I warned him. Now look."

Nerys Ferris lingered in The Pit longer than most, face pale and powdered, hair, once strawberry blonde, now behaving like hydrangea in oscillating from pink to blue and back again, blooming in perverse opposition to the tint of coiffure sported by neighbour Dot Borthwick.

At the fag end of her days, rocking on the verandah at midnight, addressing an audience of working class ghosts, Nerys Ferris promoted the view that blow-in Herbert Hobbs, son of teacher *Hobbsie*, retired regional banker, home renovator, four-wheel driver, white-clad-wife rarely seen, was conducting an affair with local conservationist Mrs Greenie Fucking Blow-In. Nerys Ferris had seen them talking, swore on The Bible she had heard the words fossil fuel, pollution and condom, and ventured to suggest that perhaps Herbert, Mrs Greenie Fucking Blow-In, and Herbert's white-dressed woman-wife, might constitute *a green threesome*. Her lips moving, a soft, wet whistle the only sound forthcoming, Nerys Ferris heard, loudly, every word she said.

The Queen Of The Pit died early the next morning. Her death was discovered two days later by Dot Borthwick.

Dimity Dilys, resident in Bangkok, stewardess for an Asian airline, arranged long distance for her mother's ashes to be scattered in the creek behind the cottage. Heavy rain rendered Nerys Ferris's final destination uncertain. A metal alloy plaque on the brick Memorial Wall celebrates her life.

The Ferris home was promptly demolished by the parent company of the former mine, for real estate purposes.

CHARLES BOYD BORTHWICK
29 May 1878 – 23 December 1911
Beloved Husband of Alice
Father of Evelyn and Malcolm
Killed By A Runaway Skip

Charlie Borthwick had long concluded that were he to die in the pit it would be while bottom-holing, but in the end, mauled by a runaway skip in E tunnel, it was the slope which did for him. It was said he would have heard it coming, but not in time. Why Charlie, a hewer, was in the haulage way at the time of his death was never established. Alcohol was thought involved.

The notice in the *Newcastle Herald* read: *The funeral was well-attended by members of The Grand United Order Of Free Gardeners, and there were many floral tributes.*

It was said that Charlie could get sweet peas to grow up a shovel stuck in a slack heap. In defiance of foul air and the absence of town water, his garden constituted a blaze of colour, joyful and long-living, in the blackened town. There was a secret here, which by passing prematurely Charlie had failed to bequeath to his descendants, the garden all but perishing on son Malcolm's watch.

The Pit closed for half a shift on the afternoon of the burial. The names of several of Charlie's colleagues featured in next morning's newspaper. Attested by nature of crime and size of fine imposed, Lionel Thorpe appeared least able to hold alcohol, Hector Morgan the ability to hold the most, whilst Hamish Bathgate possessed the loudest and foulest mouth. The Free Gardeners, blind drunk, had, it seemed, run riot *in memoriam*.

Charlie is commemorated by a mediaeval-esque stone marker etched with a garland of blooms, Scotch Thistle at the apex. Losing definition to wind, water, salt, and the incursion of lichen, the headstone today is capable of tilting back and forth in the manner of a reclining aircraft seat. Prior to his disappearance, son Malcolm was known to enjoy terrifying offspring Dorothy and Ronald with the assertion that, late at night, Grampa might emerge from the earth to sit, tilt back, and survey with disapproval the landscape of a dead working class.

ALICE MARY BORTHWICK
born 3 August 1882, Elsecar, Yorkshire
died 17 June, 1939
Beloved Mother of Evelyn and Malcolm
Grandmother of Dorothy and Ronald
All That Is Solid Melts Into Air

Alice Mary Borthwick, née Rankine – 'Gramma' – was a Barnsley lass. Coal was in the blood. Her grandmother, as a girl a *hurrier*, crawled on hands and knees, topless, dragging a coal tram on a chain between her legs, while her sister, a *shunter*, shoved the tram from behind with her forehead, and lost the front of her hair.

"They sent little children down pit too, until Huskar. Twenty-six dead." Migrating in 1894, fifty years of sunlight, sea water and detached cottages on grassy ground wrought negligible change in Gramma. The West Riding clung to her grimly. A letterful of bad news would arrive from Barnsley every month. Gramma kept a scrapbook. Statistics too were in the blood. Dutifully the black-clad matriarch took on board the darker arithmetic of antipodean coal mining. Mt Kembla. Firedamp. Ninety-six dead. South Bulli. Eighty-one dead. Bellbird. Twenty-one. Wonthaggi. Thirteen.

Tradition mandated that chronicles of exploitation, rebellion, workingman's history, mine craft, would pass from father to son whilst working together at the coalface. Charlie Borthwick's premature demise derailed communication of the legacy to son Malcolm.

Despite serial endeavour and deep knowledge of the subject, Gramma found to her dismay that the detail and gravitas of pit heritage could not be transmitted to a boy, in the home, by a widowed mother. Thus, Gramma believed, Malcolm had grown up *soft*.

Her discovery that daughter Evelyn, at fifteen, was with child, also dismayed. A Hexham woman who made home visits sorted out the situation. Deploying arithmetic and a calendar, Gramma ascertained the identity of the father, but kept what had occurred from the rest of the family. The significance of Eve's obsessional stalking up and down the creekbed, her attempted interment of newborn baby nephew Ronald at the foot of a paperbark on the creek bank, on April 25, 1925, thus eluded them. It was quite possible the significance also eluded Eve. On a later Anzac Day, in the throes of senile volubility, Gramma was heard through closed bedroom door to round ferociously on her brother, Bill Rankine, M.M. Uncle Bill had perished at Pozières. Gramma spent the entirety of Anzac Day hissing at his ghost, declaring him a cowardly bastard and vowing to scratch his name off the school Honour Roll, with her fingernails if she had to. Sister continued to give brother holy hell long after the sun had gone down. Evelyn is reported to lie in Greta Cemetery, in an unmarked grave.

Failing to heed a dinner call, Gramma Borthwick was discovered perched on the edge of the bed, knitting to hand, staring at the window as though Uncle Bill was outside, looking in. In the words of grandson Ronald:

"I tapped her on the shoulder and her head flopped. I buried her in the Kirk quarter. Eve got the bed to herself.

Gramma lay there for forty years, quiet as a mouse, until Arthur Scargill took on Margaret Thatcher. Then, if you put your ear to the ground, I swear you could hear Gramma spinning in her grave. It'd been a shit forty years. Pits were getting closed down everywhere. Now the fightback was on. In the UK, anyway. Where did the strike begin? Cortonwood Pit, south of Barnsley, where Gramma hailed from. I walked off the graveyard in sympathy. Going to the pub in sympathy made sense.

Anyway, it all went down the crapper. Thatcher got the chocolates, Arthur holed up in a house the NUM had paid for and refused to talk, the UK miners went back down to pass whatever time was left before the pits closed for good. Gramma drilled her way to the surface and stalked out of the fog in her long black dress yowling that the NUM defeat was the beginning of the end, then strode off into The Pit to haunt Mrs Greenie Fucking Blow-In and bourgeois dickhead Herbert Hobbs and anyone else opposed to coal and coal miners, and hound and bark at them forevermore on behalf of the boys who would now never work beside their fathers who worked beside their fathers who worked beside their fathers. Gramma Borthwick loved coal."

Eschewing decoration as flippant, if not popish, the Borthwick matriarch's memorial combines the humility of The Kirk with the temerity of Marx and Engels, a comingling generally unwelcome to both faiths, but successfully accommodated by Gramma throughout her life and, should she have had her way, thereafter.

The passing of Gramma Borthwick cleared the way for grandson Ronald to relocate his father's memorial from Presbyterian to Anglican, there to keep company with onetime wife Sarah and neighbouring onetime parents-in-law.

RONALD CHARLES BORTHWICK
22.9.1925 – 1.4.1985

In his pomp, Ronald Borthwick sported a bushfire of red hair, milk-white skin constellated in freckles, and pale lashes fringing translucent pink lids upon eyes the grey of overcast sky, all of which foretold a life to be eked away from sunlight. *Born to mine*, it was remarked, as had been remarked of earlier Borthwicks, historically red-haired, the recessive trait of which Ronald carried to hitherto unseen extremes. The first fiery tendrils had shocked even his father, Malcolm, profound redhead and known card who, proudly outdone, declared:

"Your great grandfather and grandfather had red hair. I have red hair. But you have the reddest hair of all, son. You are the culmination of the great and longstanding tradition of red-haired Borthwick coalminers, none of whom ever had a clue why they worked in the pit."

Ronald's education tended inadvertent. His hair, choice of seating – rear of classroom – and attraction to scenery and events outside the nearest window, confirmed him as a *born troublemaker*. A serial querying of orthodoxy underpinned a schooling largely spent in attainment of a duster-scarred head. The hurling of blackboard dusters at errant pupils was considered legitimate discipline at the time. Notably troubling to the *born troublemaker* was a seeming contradiction between education and the hewing of coal, manifest in depiction of the pit head on the school badge. The dignity of labour he determined highly suspect. Any thought of avoiding industrial destiny was scuttled at age nine by the disappearance of his father. Had *making trouble* been directed to service

of the working class, Ronald Borthwick might have become a promi-
nent figure in the industrial struggle. His claiming of responsibility for
smuggling beer into the Stay-In of 1941, in protective loyalty to actual
culprit Jimmy, chalky-boned, about to be thrashed boneless, facilitated
Ronald's graduation, at sixteen, from *born troublemaker* to *class enemy*.

Six months following expulsion from the pit, queueing at Swansea
Council Chambers to pay arrears on his father's burial plot, a chance
encounter with Stan Smith enlisting for war resulted in Ronald's
anointment as local gravedigger for the duration. In a second stroke of
good fortune, the Miners Federation and the Undertakers Assistants
and Cemetery Employees Union did not share blacklists. The cemetery also furnished fellow pariah Jimmy a testing ground for the lawnmower gifted by undermanager Goldfinch. Pressed as to Goldfinch
having promoted the planting of beer during the Stay-In, Jimmy
laughed, said *the machines* were coming, and that there would soon be
a motorised device for digging graves.

The flame-haired ferryman to the souls of The Pit did not limit
himself to digging and filling graves. He weeded unsealed barrows.
He restored floral tributes scattered by wind or trampled by dogs.
He cleaned dirty jam jars housing flora. He repainted timber crosses.
Corrected spelling. Straightened headstones worked loose in friable ground. Restored fallen statuary. Replaced stolen votive offer-
ings. Polished plaques. Swept sand. Collected dogshit. These tasks
he undertook in late-affirmed embrace of *solidarity*. Blacklisting, he
became convinced, did not preclude solidarity. Shovelling, it would
more than once occur that were he to continue beyond the traditional
six feet, his excavation would sooner or later connect with a branch-
line of the pit. He therefore remained, in his mind, a miner, of sorts.
Thus, hurling shovel, pick, and crowbar to the bottom of incomplete

excavations into which bereaved relatives might have expected to deposit Tommy Sim, Old Davey Owen, Gareth Davies, Barry Toohey and Hector Morgan, had not their various demises been coincident with strike activity, Ronald in industrial sympathy would abandon work-in-progress and walk off the cemetery. Relatives were in the main accepting of the show of solidarity, while turning a blind eye to Ronald's alcoholic crossing of his own picket line, late at night, the pub having closed, to attempt completion of their particular digging. The General Strike of 1949, lasting seven weeks, tested commitment. Ronald's mother, echoing Gramma Borthwick, frequently reminded her son that in 1917, while his father was pelting scabs with rocks and being bashed by police, Prime Minister Chifley, then a striking railwayman, found himself placed on a black list: "Never to be re-employed". The lesson to be learned, if there was one, evaded Ronald.

Loyalty proving a *leitmotif*, the viewing of Nerys Ferris *in flagrante* with undermanager-turned-overmanager Willy Goldfinch did not deter Ronald's continued acceptance that he and Nerys Ferris were, at her insistence, made for each other, despite nothing intimate occurring between them for over fifty years. That Jimmy had prior knowledge of the liaison and so was able to escort Ronald to witness the coupling in the sand dunes did not greatly perturb him. Jimmy always seemed to have a finger on the pulse.

There was to be a second, more mercurial love of Ronald's life: Maria Vella, niece of pit ostler Alberto 'Wingnut' Vella. Romance flowering on a memorable afternoon spent at the first postwar Sydney Royal Easter Show in 1947, and over the ensuing evening in the Bellevue Private Hotel (For Single Gentlemen Only) deep in Surry Hills, the relationship was over by early morning. Venturing late night to the hotel kitchen to purloin beer, Ronald returned to find Maria gone,

Jimmy in tears explaining that he had taken issue with Maria over her disparagement of Ronald's first sexual endeavour with the pejorative *dud root*. Jimmy's defence of his mate's honour had stimulated Maria to cast further aspersions upon both their manhoods, then to seize Jimmy's wrist, break it, and depart. Incompletely persuaded, Ronald searched nearby Central Railway, adjacent bus stops and streets, in vain. Brandy was waiting for him upon his return to the hotel. She was nineteen, she said, smelt of musk and rum, and had run into Jimmy earlier, in East Sydney. Subsequent to the Bellevue Hotel incident, back in The Pit, 'Wingnut' Vella shirtfronted Ronald with notice that his niece had returned to Malta and violence would follow any attempt to contact the island. Maria lingered in Ronald's mind a lifetime, but the more he drank, the more he afforded Jimmy's description of events that night the benefit of the doubt.

Alcohol was observed to have agency, from prodigiously early days, in Ronald's progress from *born troublemaker* to *suspected strike saboteur* to *class enemy* to *recidivist perpetrator of social atrocity*. His father's best mate, 'Jockey' Mayfield, had in an act of mateship slipped toddler Ronald his first taste of black, a seven ounce glass, while Malcolm was taking a leak. Thereafter Jockey would slip the boy a taste every time Malcolm sat him on the bar. Ronald was *a regular* by the age of eighteen months.

As, dazedly, by torchlight, he sought the shotgun on the final evening, it was clear, as clear as anything ever was in his later life, especially after the day he had just had, the daze in which it had left him, that 1949 had been the beginning of the end. General Strike undone by a Labor Government only months before, he had been bailing an early summer evening's downpour from the future resting place of Joe Keats when the issue of *Popular Mechanics* splashed down beside him, to float open at a feature on the invention, by Vaino J. Holopainen and

47

Roy E. Handy Jr, of the first hydraulic backhoe. There had been no need for Jimmy to say "Told you so," but he had said it. More than once. Ronald had forcefully attempted to promote the view that "a soul would not rest in a hole dug by machine," but Jimmy would have none of it. The magazine had refused to sink. The inventors had formed the Wain-Roy Corporation to market their machine worldwide.

Ronald and the coal pit would be seen to decline in tandem. As mechanisation killed off labour two miles underground[3], Ronald six feet down was in time supplanted by a descendant of Holopainen and Handy Jr's rear-mounted digger, at the machine's controls "a spotty Charlestown blow-in with no respect." Again there had been no need for Jimmy to say "Told you so" but he had. By the time of his enforced departure from the field, Ronald had buried almost everyone he knew.

The waning of the pit was deemed calamitous. Ronald's parallel downward trajectory was adjudged a spectacle. So spectacular as to become live entertainment for former tormentors and overturn the *suspected strike saboteur's* proscription from pub and club. Majorly obese, in the sway of alcoholism, the former exile would, oft-times without prompting, perform *The Dance of The Flaming Arseholes* atop a bowling club table. He would make concerted attempt on the Guinness Record for retaining a live cat down a pair of shorts, the garment being worn at the time. He would remove bloated, long-dead greyhounds from the bottom of backyard wells, mummified flying foxes from clogged gully traps, and transistor radios tuned to sporting stations from the dark depths of thunderpit toilets. His reward, liquor, of any kind, of any quality, of any volume. The regime, rigorous, was

[3]Samson arc-wall and Jeffrey B35 crawler-mounted cutters could slice twenty-three-foot arcs , nine feet deep, into the bord face, in four minutes. Electric borers holed nine feet between cuts. Crawler-mounted Joy loaders filled skips. Battery-powered locomotives transported miners. Machinery being new, seniority was discounted and management selected men.

complemented by irregular consumption of raw eggs and satisfaction of a sweet tooth with bakery confections. The pit would cough along for a further thirty years before being put out of its misery.

The final resting place of Ronald Borthwick, B21, is a shambles: breathtakingly untended, stabbed by a flimsy wooden cross, its horizontal arm held by single loosening nail and destined to fly in a stiff breeze, if not by time of writing having already flown. That the hand which undertook the painting of Ronald's name was demonstrably unsteady has led to speculation, in light of subsequent misadventure involving a shotgun, that in a rare instance of pre-planning on his part, the hand was Ronald's own. Dot Borthwick visits her brother's grave on his birthday.

(Dot celebrated her own, one-hundredth birthday on March 11, 2024. She attributes her longevity to "cigarettes, sherry, and never marrying" and continues to occupy the family cottage with daughter Shelley.)

WILLIAM EDWARD BURNS
16 November 1907 – 2 March 1957
You'll Do

Billy Burns' Wigan accent would thicken noticeably as he wound his way back, *in memoriam*, to the High Brooks and Ince Hall collieries where explosions of firedamp had accounted for thirty-seven miners, including Jeremiah Burns, and fifteen miners, including John Burns, respectively. Locating a second wind, Billy would oft-times move on to the Bickershaw colliery and a lift cage accident where nineteen men fell five-hundred dark yards to their deaths, drowned in the pit sump, whence Billy would assert that he was a lucky man, having been a shiftman in Bickershaw at the time. Pausing for effect, the Wigan expat would then whistle an extended descending note in illustration of a heavy object plummeting to earth.

Easily lubricated, Billy was a man of many words, all highly familiar to comrades from regular rotation, but listening to him passed the time.

Billy claimed to have *in scroom* bitten off the ear of a rugby league prop from Hull in the days when Billy had teeth. Had the prop hailed from St Helen's, Billy bellowed, a curiously high-pitched and bird-like bellow, accompanied by dripping gums, he would have bitten off both ears. Billy then would cackle like a frayed squeeze box, toddle to the window, spit clear over the verandah rail despite his shortness of stature, and announce "I were King of Friggin' Wigan. Abdicated to experience dignity of labour. Friggin' Wigan!"

Billy also taught novices how to open a beer bottle with an eye socket. Having himself left mastery of the skill too late, in consequence suffering dental damage, he had, he avowed, formed an intent to save the teeth of the younger generation.

Further, Billy had a pet theory on the mysterious disappearance of Malcolm Borthwick: Malcolm had not drowned, nor been taken by a shark, Malcolm had *run away*. From The Pit, from family, from working class fate. Whereupon Billy would reveal for the umpteenth time that he, Billy, might know of *another* miner – no names, no pack drill – who may also have *run away*. Thirty years before. Abandoning a family in Wigan. Billy would then wink, severally, before revealing that the unnamed fellow in question had *another* family now.

Billy died of the dust. His local widow, Ida, attended the funeral. His other widow, Shirley, ex Wigan, now Rotherham, having crossed the Pennines to remarry in haste, was unavailable. During the 1984-85 UK Miners' Strike, one of Shirley Burns' sons by her second husband was injured at 'The Battle of Orgreave', when mounted police charged miners' picket lines.

Billy Burns' burial mound has turned a bald patch of flat, stony earth, resistant to vegetation. Domestic jars housing dead flowers and plastic blooms, model motor vehicles, inexplicable children's toys and football team devotional objects, add colour.

METHODIST

HENRY VERNON HOBBS
4 February 1898 – 6 May 1948
At Rest At Last

Henry Hobbs – 'Hobbsie' to those he attempted to teach – was a quiet Department of Education communist who welcomed a first posting to the one-room school of The Pit as a two-way educative engagement with the working class. Depiction of the pit head on the school badge he saw as emblematic of his challenge.

On day one, exiting in a state of exhilaration, Henry discovered his bicycle stripped of parts, its frame wedged immovably in a cleft of the storm-blasted Monterey Pine dominating the dirt playground. The frame, over time, would become part of the tree. Evening brought discovery of a flaming paper bag on Henry's front stoop, inducing a flurry of stomping prior to the realisation of upon what, inside the bag, he was stomping.

On day two a *troika* of disruptives, Ronald Borthwick, Jimmy Treloar and Cedric Keats, identified as the principal obstacle to Henry's debunking of the notion of limited working-class horizons, and implantation of other possibilities. Disdaining mere disinterest in learning, the *troika* gravitated to open rebellion, gleefully shepherding classmates into the fray.

Day three confirmed that the challenge to theories of environmental disadvantage, the battle against futility, would be constant.

Henry's Waterloo arrived with The Empire Day Incident of May 24, 1939. The national flag, ascending, came to an unexplained halt at half-mast; three coal-grimed but familiar figures appeared bearing a home-made coffin; the casket deposited at the school gates, the student assembly dashed to the fence in riotous humour; Dot Borthwick trilled a version of 'The International'; Nerys Ferris hurdled the barrier, threw herself upon the casket, sobbed at volume and overdid the role of widow; the tallest pallbearer intoned a eulogy:

"Here lie the mortal remains of John Smith. Who worked hard and died poor, supported throughout the trials and vicissitudes of life by the reflection that he was the proud inheritor of a share in the glorious empire upon which the sun never sets. At his death he was placed in this grave and his share of the glorious empire was reverently shovelled on top of him so that he came by his own in the end."

The pallbearers duly hurled handfuls of earth atop the coffin and fled. The oath of allegiance, "I honour my God, I serve my Queen, I salute the flag", was not taken. Three pupils remained in formal assembly: Henry's son, Herbert, disguising amusement; management children Craig and Felicity Goldfinch, tempted to join the insurrection but held back by class upbringing. Cedric Keats was fingered as the mastermind, Ronald Borthwick the mastermind behind the mastermind. The ensuing *Cracker Night* was more explosive than ever. John Smith's 'eulogy' was sourced to a 1921 trial issue of *Common Cause*, the Miners Federation newspaper, in the possession of Cedric's father, Joe Keats.

Mr Hobbs explained that the subsequent mass caning did not indicate personal disapproval of uprisings, but that there was a time and a place. He did not cane the girls, instead instructing them to calculate, in their heads, how many cuts in total had been administered in the session. Girls wrongly calculating the product of twenty-three times six were detained after school and made to read a novel by

Joseph Conrad. Three canes having splintered in the administration of one hundred and thirty-eight cuts, Mr Hobbs further instructed his female pupils to deploy this statistic in deducing the average hits per cane before occurrence of splintering. Mr Hobbs then asked, if he possessed a total of twenty canes, how many cuts could he administer before running out of canes?

Henry enjoyed several years of friendship with Alec Gemmell, pursued in a quieter corner of the pub, before departing The Pit for the relief of foreign climes in 1941.

A postcard to Alec confirmed internment in Singapore, by the Japanese. Henry died six weeks after repatriation.

He lies beneath light grey granite, green-veined in certain light, the memorial, commissioned by Alec Gemmell, proportioned to the golden mean. Ronald Borthwick spoke at the lowering. That the actions of his worst-behaved pupils may have been *examinations* of his commitment to an ignored and disdained community never occurred to Henry.

REGINALD JOHN WORSELY

12 January 1900 – 17 October 1969

Kept The Faith

Reg Worsley's great grandfather Silas migrated from the West Midlands to look for gold in and around Bathurst, but found only coal, in Lithgow, at two shillings and six pence a ton. Joining a small community of refugee miners from the Black Country residing in slab and mud huts and tents surrounding the mine, Silas and descendants went on to become stalwarts of industrial agitation in the Vale of Clwydd pit.

Underground by fourteen, cavilled out at fifteen under the aegis of *last in, first out*, to the relief of management who knew a budding socialist firebrand when they saw one, Reg moved east, over the mountains, and found work on the northern fields.

Turning seventeen in 1917, Reg found himself perfectly situated for emotional connection with the Russian Revolution. That three months later, in Hartley End, Staffordshire, one hundred and fifty five miners perished in the Minnie Pit only strengthened Reg's conviction that the answer to Lenin's question "What Is To Be Done?" had been found, and further, that his great grandfather's decision to seek gold in the antipodes, instead of coal in Staffordshire, may well have saved himself and several other family members from contributing to the death toll at Minnie Pit.

'Red Reg' had no sense of humour discernible to others. His adherence to the writings of Marx was biblical. Faced with an industrial/political/economic problem he would ask: what would Karl say?

57

Should no answer be immediately forthcoming, Reg would scour *The Complete Works* and invariably find it. Spreading the word, he conducted classes in Marxism at the Wallsend Mechanics Institute, lessons noted for ideological rigour and intolerance of lateness. Reg had no truck with dissent. Straying brought down anathema. The mature Marxist did later see clear to an accommodation of Lenin and Stalin as flawed but practical individuals who, in deviating, were simply ignorant or misguided, and whose actions in the long run were but insignificant detours from the path of the inevitable progress of historical materialism.

Mid century, General Strike defeated, nationalisation not occurring, machines coming onto pillars, output rocketing from *critical shortage* in 1950 to *oversupply* in 1952, communists routinely outvoted in the Miners Federation, the Labor Party splitting, cavils out every year from 1955 to 1960, inclusive, Reg was forced to concede that the inevitable progress of historical materialism did not seem to be the way things were panning out. He further concluded it was the disciples, always the disciples, who buggered things up.

Reginald Worsley rests beneath what appears a concrete recliner. Of heavy, dark, granular material, seemingly half sunk in the earth, the commemorative cannot be said to sit lightly upon its site. A touch of art deco may be detected in the stepped shoulders of the headstone, and what seem to be curved, stunted armrests. The Worsley family name is given on a plaque at the toe of the slab, Reginald's details on the headstone. A metal-grated slot at the toe allows the disposition of flowers. Grandchildren have been photographed atop the memorial, smiling, hands clasped behind head, legs stretched, reclining.

According to gravedigger Ronald Borthwick, Reginald's location in Methodist was attributable to typographical error or possibly, less accidentally, to family belief that it was never too late.

LIONEL BALTHAZAR THORPE
2 February 1887 – 23 September 1952
Here Lies A Derby Man

Lionel's workday face was a black planet in midst of which oscillated a pair of eyeballs, frantic, in raspberry-rimmed sockets. Lionel had nystagmus. A nocturnal Methodist and staunch Bolshevik, he focused on the similarities – embrace of the working class, dignity of labour, personal discipline, organisation – and ignored the contradictions. If one system failed, Lionel had back up in the other. He cackled without smiling. His long black fingers pointed like arrows. Sober, frowning upon dancing, the morning after a church social saw Lionel turn to communism for the antidote to guilt.

Lionel was a contract man. Time was money. Following shot firing, dust in the bord nowhere near cleared, Lionel and Hec Morgan, hewing mates of long standing, would scamper like gnomes into the cloud of dust to rip coal. Both lived longer than comrades expected.

Two miles of more or less solid earth underground, Lionel pro-claimed the ability to pinpoint, with dark arrowing finger, at any moment in time, the precise location of the sun overhead. Money had changed hands in verification of this ability. Lionel also claimed, when working one of the many veins honeycombing deep offshore, to be able to hear waves breaking overhead. Viewing sunlight and sea as breeding dangerous relaxation of mind and spirit, the Derbyshire man yearned to return to the midlands, but in vain, his extensive family not sharing their patriarch's longing for leaden skies, dank streets and foul smells. That he hankered for a drizzling home but remained on the sunny side of the earth, Lionel was forced to conclude, evidenced an abhorrent state of pleasure in sin.

In expressing mortification at his sinfulness, Lionel's Derby roots might frequently be heard to deepen and spread across and under the county, his basso rumbling through the streets of historic Chesterfield where resided any number of coalmining Thorpes, including John Thorpe, one of twenty-six to perish in the 1871 explosion of firedamp at the Renishaw Park colliery.

The first Balthazar Thorpe, christened after one of The Magi in the hope of bettering the family fortunes, was transported to Australia for theft. Colonial sunshine in the form of a melanoma took Lionel Thorpe.

He lies in site C14, unidentified, a tinplate marker on a wooden cross corroded beyond legibility through the action of sun and salt water.

OWEN DAVID JONES

Born 12 December 1898

Departed This Life 5 February 1964

Cwm Rhondda

There being innumerable Joneses on the northern coalfields, these seams tending nonconformist protestant, and more than several Jones, Owens, Owen Jones of The Pit found himself specified 'Short' Owen Jones, he resembling an oversized bath toy in a shabby suit beneath which he regularly went shirtless. The pit being a contract pit, Short Owen walked on short legs with a briskness few could match. In amusement, he would roar and shake like a tickled toad.

Living up to stereotype, at times exceeding it, Short Owen was able to maintain perfect pitch under duress, his tenor rippling with beauty even in company of a less talented, inebriated chorus. A preferred vocalist at funerals, at the pub his sweet tones would routinely form glissandi over the evening as it grew late. West Cessnock, regular Eisteddfod winners, had several times attempted to poach him but Short Owen was solid.

Joneses Short Owen, Dickie, Johnno, and Neville, supplemented at times by a cohort of drinkers from pits further afield, in the main surnamed Davis, Davies, Davy, Dodds, Evans, Hughes, Jenkins, Morgan, Roberts, Thomas and Williams, would often, under the influence, be heard melodically to return to assorted home vales, with frequent sidetracks up the Rhymney to pay respects at Senghenydd – which only they could pronounce – where of the record four hundred and thirty-nine who died in 1913, forty-four were named Jones. Or at times, while treading the valley of the Taff, to burrow into the anthracite of Merthyr Vale, nearby Aberfan, and the highest rates of black lung, contracted at a younger age, within the United Kingdom.

Wife Gwen having died giving birth to son Neville, widower Short Owen fell to longtime courtship of putative widow Sarah Borthwick, her marital status in flux while the fate of her husband remained indeterminate. Short Owen was not to live long enough to witness the full repercussions of his gifting a shotgun to Sarah's son Ronald. Nevertheless, he did in short time come to believe it was something he might not have done, given the eventual marriage to Sarah lasted six months, the couple returning to Australia, from Wales, on separate ships.

In retirement, Short Owen became a stalwart of the lawn bowls team. That he could sing and bowl at the same time unsettled opposition teams.

Short Owen Jones lies beneath a raised garden bed, walled by concrete blocks, wherein sprout a variety of weeds from a bed of coal-coated pebbles. Numerous relatives rest nearby in a historically informative Jones precinct. While Mayfields and Gemmells were to vie for most men underground, the Joneses buried the most women.

NEVILLE BLEDDYN JONES
b 23 January 1927 – d 18 June 1988
He Sings With The Choir Of Angels

After a difficult birth, his mother dying in the process, Neville Jones grew to thrive, rising to Captain of The Pit Volunteer Fire Brigade, with an unofficial sideline as weekend firebug. An uneasy relationship with wife Sheila presenting soon after marriage, shifts in the pit parted the couple during the working week, while regular local bushfires served to keep Neville out of the house on weekends. The arrangement suited both parties. More than a few spouses in The Pit were heard to encourage the regular call outs of their men. The curl of gum-scented smoke on a weekend afternoon was reassuring notice that Neville and crew were on the job. The extramural activity would become a darker issue with the 1970 Captain Cook Bicentennial Burn-off, 'Black Sunday'.

The Wyong dog track enabled additional weekend absenteeism. A keen punter, Neville remained a lifelong subscriber to the *Greyhound Recorder*, despite the organ proving of no assistance in the picking of winners. The publication could always be put to use in starting a fire. Neville was never admitted to the cabal of local punters *in the know* as to the mercurial form of bookie's nemesis, Mystery Man.

Further absence from home and hearth was enjoyed through invention of himself as the prime mover in construction, by himself and fellow miners facing premature retirement, of a lawn bowling club resembling a giant fibro shoebox atop a hill. Revelation of the dangers

63

of asbestos found Neville leading the way in concealing the club's original cladding behind profiled aluminium sheeting.

The regular maintenance of the club facilities also drew Neville's attention away from matters domestic. Rolling the links, the rhythm, reminded him of youthful wheeling days in the pit. Post stroke, Neville remained a club fixture, seated with a good sightline to the racing channels, spilling Tia Maria and milk down the front of his whites.

Cremated in Broadmeadow, it was remarked at the wake that reduction to ash was an apt conclusion to Neville's career in local fire. While not the first of The Pit to undergo cremation, those preceding him had afterwards been scattered to the winds, at times with unfortunate results, and remained physically uncommemorated. Neville was the first local deceased to be celebrated via metal alloy plaque mounted on a squat, cream brick Memorial Wall, this edifice, over time, with the accumulation of additional plaques, coming to resemble the letterbox row outside a mid-twentieth century block of flats.

In commemoration of the stray ember which had rendered his recently-fledged pet galah near featherless, Ronald Borthwick christened the charred bird Neville. Roosting on the verandah rail, the bird under tutelage promptly learned to remind passers by of the reason for his lack of plumage below the neck: *"Black Sunday! Black Sunday!"*

WILLIAM BERNARD GOLDFINCH
4 June 1895 – 30 July 1967
He Lived To Serve

Businessman ex The Ruhr, post turn of century seeking improved prospects across The Channel, a prescient Wolfgang Stieglitz saw fit to anglicise the family name fully two years before the German army crossed the Belgian border, and further, to secure employment within a small precinct, up north, where there would be less chance of his former self being remembered or unearthed. Son Wilhelm Bernhard Stieglitz thus became William Bernard Goldfinch. Willy's marriage to Sunderland ship captain's daughter Adrienne, the rapid production of children Craig and Felicity, diligent embrace of Methodism, finalised the transition to full Englishman.

Willy wore a black hat, a brown suit, stiff Egyptian cotton handkerchief monogrammed 'W.G.' protruding from the pocket, and saw himself a soft cop as regards his dealings with the industrial workforce. Identifying post-Victorian, wanting to be liked, Willy had determined on the voyage to Australia that he would not live up to the toffee-nosed bullying stereotype of industrial management, but rather, would be firm but fair to English, Scots, Irish, and Welshmen alike. Arrival in The Pit as mine undermanager saw this balance sorely tested, not least upon encountering a number of Maltese men working in the pit, all of whom, at first glance, appeared politically fractious. Then there were the Italians. Willy expeditiously dispensed with suit and hat.

Management and philandering historically having been found a natural fit, Willy Goldfinch concluded he was not one to argue with history. Promoting liaison with widow Betty Treloar by securing her son work above ground, Willy perceived additional benefit in the education of young Jimmy on the industrial struggle from the management point of view. Jimmy learned that without coal, there would be no civilization, for civilization had been built on coal. He learned that coal miners had Willy Goldfinch's respect and admiration, the undermanager, however, admitting to concern that a minority of *red raggers* were *white-anting* Australian civilization in the service of foreign masters, and that this was counter to the freedom for which he, Willy Goldfinch, would have fought in the Great War, had he not been declared medically unfit. For which side he would have battled remained unmentioned. Willy further instructed Jimmy in the benefits of mechanisation, laying particular stress on management's awareness of the safety aspect, all the while detailing his understanding of the men's need for job security, how he too desired security of employment, and the manner in which history had proven that the only security was *progress*. Jimmy learned that The Pit was finished if the mine stood still, and he, Willy Goldfinch, would not let that happen.

Willy's relationship with Nerys Ferris, she seventeen – or sixteen? – was pursued covertly, outdoors, by night, until the upward mobility of his secretary to ensconcement atop Snob Hill was found impossible to conceal. Nerys Ferris's subsequent hasty descent and the return of wife Adrienne saw Willy, after a brief second honeymoon, secure a transfer to the Metropolitan Pit on the southern coalfields. He once more discarded Adrienne, and this time, upon being taken to the cleaners in the divorce settlement, Craig and Felicity, along with other belongings.

Willy discovered managerial work in the south closely to resemble that in the north. Perhaps, probably, it was worse. He did not enjoy distributing retrenchment notices. In the post-war decades of mechanisation and overproduction, loss of markets, competition from oil, brief recovery followed by worse collapse, it seemed the putting off of men, the occasional putting back on, only to put off again, was all Willy did. He found the actuality of *laissez faire* (or thereabouts), emotionally exhausting. He was happy to take early retirement.

Divorce proceeds enabled the relocation of Adrienne and the Goldfinch children to an inner-city terrace house in Sydney, left in poor condition by former working-class occupants, but with potential. Unencumbered, Willy found himself bemusedly embracing the notion of passing retirement in The Pit. The populace was down to earth. Self-sufficient. He liked that. No longer being management, he mused, perhaps his relationship with fellow residents would be different. He returned with sufficient to purchase the cottage which once housed Lionel Thorpe and family, and renovate to taste.

Class consciousness had not yet withered away. In the wake of incidents involving former employees, Willy opted not to patronise bowling club and pub. He fished and watched television. Read German history and traced his ancestry. Out walking, he would cross the street upon spying Nerys Ferris and/or Dimity Dilys. Confronted by Reg Worsley or one or more retired, red-ragging Gemmells, he would strenuously deny labelling as *wreckers of civilization* the striking men of 1941, let alone to a newspaper man describing coal miners as *leftist troublemakers who did not know their place, which was to provide civilization with power, light and heat, and not complain,* and vehemently protest innocence to the charge of bribing *suspected strike saboteurs* Ronald Borthwick and Jimmy Treloar to smuggle beer into the pit, down the contents, position empties in a location pre-arranged for management in the form of himself to 'stumble upon', broadcast details of the unsavoury goings-on underground far and wide above ground, and so facilitate the caricaturing of the Stay-In as a *Miners Underground Picnic, Red Strikers Booze-up!*, and worse, by an antagonistic city press.

Willy Goldfinch died in a Newcastle nursing home. His grave asserts reticence underpinned by a Teutonic stolidity. His particulars are inscribed on one page of an open book fashioned in white marble. The other page remains blank. Perhaps not wishing to be disturbed, perhaps still class conscious, his resting place is enclosed within a waist-high spear-ended wrought-iron fence.

LEWIS LLEWELLYN PHILLIPS
9.8.1921 – 15.7.2012
'Fizzer'

"Fucking come on! Fucking come on you bastard! You bastard! You bastard!"

The screech of shot-firer 'Fizzer' Phillips encouraging a damp taper was high tradition in The Pit. Several water sources were overhead, in eastern sections the Tasman Sea, The Pit was *a wet pit*. Fizzer Phillips managed to produce significantly more and damper tapers than any other shot firer.

"Fucking come on you bastard! You bastard! You bastard!"

Fizzer Phillips also specialised in missed shots which, left uncleared, might later explode in a hewer's face. How Fizzer gained entry to night school, let alone attain a Deputy's ticket, was a daily source of scatalogical consternation.

Shot firing without the prerequisite of nous had rendered Fizzer acutely deaf.

Between oaths, all shift, he would over and over whistle the same semi-melody which he himself could not hear and workmates could never identify.

Early in the war, the sighting of a U-boat surfacing east of The Pit was reported by an unidentified source. The converted liner *Queen Elizabeth*, in Sydney to pick up troops and thought to make a juicy target for torpedoes, a Wirraway was despatched from Williamtown to investigate. The Pit loading jetty crawled with heavily armed locals. Fizzer Phillips blew the head off a surfacing cormorant he took for a periscope. Sudden explosions, close to the face, had also rendered Fizzer's eyesight less than exact.

Like many miners, Fizzer was politically *left agnostic*. If communist union officials gleaned him more money and better conditions, he would vote for them. Fizzer was invariably among the first to scent which way the wind was blowing, and turn.

The death of son Geoffrey at eighteen catalysed the departure of wife Myrna for pastures less grim or, given her husband, it was remarked, less whacko. A Myrna Phillips is reportedly buried in Stockton Cemetery, Newcastle, amid numerous former steelworkers.

Fizzer Phillips observed every one of his peers *cross the white bridge* before him. A solitary fixture in Retired Miners Corner, he became a tourist attraction of sorts.

He departed life direct from The Corner, descending with glacial slowness from the dedicated Retired Miners pew to lie on the floor, behold a vision of his dead mother calling from behind an old timber fence, and die. His grave is unmarked, a southerly buster having uprooted the timber cross and deposited it, along with the markers of numerous former workmates, in parts unknown.

GEOFFREY BEVAN PHILLIPS
30.3.1941 – 5.7.1959
Born To Ride

Geoff Phillips died aboard a 1951 Harley Davidson 750WR, overtaking a turning coal truck with a faulty indicator not far from the Wangi power station where Geoff had worked since being cavilled out of The Pit in 1958. For his part, Geoff had been happy to be rationalised as he no longer had to work beside the dangerous old goat that was Fizzer Phillips, his father.

The funeral procession, a hundred or so bikers, most on Harleys, behind reflective sunglasses and bandanas, rode through The Pit, slowly, five or six abreast, on both sides of the street, emitting an ear-splitting racket and forcing coal trucks onto the footpath. Geoff's coffin, black, embellished with a red skull going up in flames and hot snakes crawling from the eye sockets, rode in a sidecar up front. It was remarked that having Fizzer Phillips for your old man would cause snakes to crawl out of anyone's eye sockets.

Geoff's father attended the funeral in a state of petrification. His mother stood well away from her husband. The balance of The Pit situated itself behind a picture window in the bowling club atop the hill to observe distant bikers behave themselves. One read a poem about freedom, another spoke of what a good mate Geoff was, another sang 'Lost Highway'. Being a still day, the dust accompanying departure of the bikes took hours to settle.

Geoff's headstone is topped by a ferro-cement rendering of a motorcycle bearing scant resemblance to the machine upon which he died.

Nevertheless, in combination with the legend 'Born To Ride', Geoff's final resting place gives strong indication that his days were numbered.

The 1958 cavil out was followed by a stay-in strike of two hundred and three hours, a new coalfields record. Two thirds of the men emerged to find themselves rationalised, management breaking their own record. Nationwide, two thousand five hundred men and thirty-three mines ceased work for good.

ROMAN CATHOLIC

SACRED TO THE MEMORY OF
DAI RICHARD JONES
12 December 1892 – 2 August 1961

GIA FRANCESCA JONES-GENIALE
21 September 1894 – 7 March 1964

LUCIA JONES-GENIALE
26 March 1914 – 20 August 1914
Our Little Angel, Taken Too Soon

ANTHONY JONES-GENIALE
Born An Angel

Gia Geniale, pencil thin, the depression of the 1890s having taken a toll, was familiar with the family rifle by the age of twelve. Rabbits and foxes her primary targets, stray men also figured in her father's instructions. Geniale males, lured from Korumburra to the new and bigger Wonthaggi pit, only returned to the Coal Creek home on Sundays. In the absence of the males, Gia and her mother share-cropped a small corner of soil owned by a fellow *pugliese* of more substantial means. Vegetables with a Mediterranean bent featured in the Sunday reunions. Neither time nor money was available to demonstrate the making of approachable wine to anglo-saxons and celts. A lager of fruity nature, tinged, as in Puglia, with prickly pear, the family found manageable.

Simultaneous with his hair being cut adjacent to the Outtrim pit by Victorian Coal Miners Association Treasurer Ernest Yardley, the militant barber having found a cutthroat razor and scissors to concentrate the mind of a potential unionist, Dai 'Dickie' Jones, fourteen, signed up to the V.C.M.A. The fledgling unionist promptly found the sins of the father visited upon him in unsuccessful applications at Outtrim, Jumbunna, Korumburra and Wonthaggi mines. Ellis Jones had been blacklisted following the 1903 Outtrim Lockout. Victimisation by proxy led Dickie to tree felling, fencing and, keen ferret acquired, rabbiting, until *Devil* shot down a tempting burrow and failed to reappear. It was presumed the animal had dined too well.

Gia and Dickie first exchanged interest at a union recruitment meeting in Wonthaggi. Gia looked good, could shoot and cook. Dickie looked good, could fell and fence, and given the opportunity, mine. Neither family encouraged further exchange. The low productivity of free labour – *scabs* – during the 'Peter Bowling strike'[4] animated the couple's elopement across the state border. The northern fields of New South Wales had, with reluctance, resumed employment of union men. His father's history appeared not to follow Dickie interstate, at least not into the isolated station that was The Pit.

The Pit pub was quickly found not to have a Ladies Lounge. Gia waited in the street. Dickie recorded two dusty flagons labelled sherry and port well to the rear of a seemingly abandoned shelf, unfortified wine there represented by a lone bottle of something entitled *claret* which, opened by the publican in curiosity, long ago, had not kept well. West of Cessnock, the publican had noted, there were winemakers, but The Pit preferred beer, of the 'old' black recipe, chased down

---

[4]Peter Bowling: President, Colliery Employees Federation, led 1909/10 strike. Arrested, placed in leg irons, spent thirty months in Goulburn Gaol. Never regained union prominence.

in times more flash by spirituous liquor. He said he would see what he could do for the new arrivals. Gia was later to find the drop from west of Cessnock quite approachable. She did not live to see wine supplant coal, if not in employment, in imagery of the region. Let alone witness the incursion of varietals from Puglia.

A propensity to organise inherited from his father first surfaced during the General Strike of 1917. Dickie thereafter rose through the ranks to election as The Pit Lodge President. As such, upon completion of the 1941 Stay-In, he paid visit to the Borthwick home to declare that, having worked with grandfather Charlie and father Malcolm, he was of firm belief that class treachery was *not* in the Borthwick blood, that Jimmy Treloar was the sole beer-smuggling *rat*, and that he, Dickie, had the numbers to see Ronald reinstated. Ronald stuck to his story. He, Ronald, was *the man with the plan*. He was not taking the rap for a mate. Jimmy confirmed his mate's testimony, swearing blind on his mother's life that Ronald was not taking the rap for him.

Gia, too, tended industrially active, her marksmanship allied with culinary skill reaching a peak of appreciation in the stew supplied to striking men, underground, in 1941. Mussolini's war, nevertheless, tested foreign relations. Gia's level of enthusiasm at *HMAS Sydney's* sinking of the *Bartolomeo Colleoni* was closely examined but found acceptable by the Miners Lodge Women's Auxiliary. Jokes about Italian tanks fitted with five reverse gears were to be tolerated, with a smile, if not overtly pronounced riotous. The hooting and dance steps on the verandah which accompanied news of Il Duce and mistress upside down in a Milanese piazza went a long way to cementing perceptions of Gia's loyalty.

Dickie Jones sang bass in The Pit Male Choir alongside Short Owen, Johnno, and Neville Jones, Mervyn Ferris, Lewis Phillips and

Hec Morgan, the ensemble supplemented by a smattering of enthusi-
astic non-Welshmen, baritones in the main. That The Pit came close
but never topped the City Of Sydney Eisteddfod podium was attributed by the Welshmen, bracingly, in the pub after the event, to choral
miscegenation. With a run up, down, Dickie could hit a very low G,
raising the question of exactly how many testicles he might possess.
One for each note lower than everyone else was a frequent suggestion.

Lucia, the couple's first child, died of whooping cough at six months.
Anthony was stillborn following an outbreak of rubella in The Pit.

Gia and Dickie lie under polished black stone, flanked by the
smaller, white graves of their infant children, the quartet lettered in
gold. Unbeliever Dickie was happy to be buried Roman Catholic.

ALAN CHRISTOPHER GOODGE

1.3.1948 – 13.7.2014

Alan, it was opined, not always out of earshot, was of that type of man who appear middle-aged all their life. Squeaky clean, giving off no odour discernible to humans, in dark suit and elastic-sided boots, the Anglo-Australian church-going solicitor had about him the aura of a clergyman who had sat too long upon cold ground.

Alan had not anticipated passing Eternity in The Pit. In the mid nineteen eighties, tipped off by a councillor that town water might soon be connected, removing the only reason the quaint, now coalmine-free hamlet had not yet become a target for the gentrifying class, Alan purchased three miners' cottages, free of miners, plus the mine accountant's residence, a superior property with hilltop views, free of accountant, only to learn that the councillor had been conducting a fifteen year liaison with Mrs Goodge and decided, finally, that Alan had to go. Town water had no intention of coming to The Pit. Mrs Goodge had no intention of staying with a man who would invest family funds so unwisely, and took their two children with her.

Determined to make the best of circumstances mysterious but arranged in heaven, Alan occupied the accountant's residence, commuted, networked, bestowed favours, working bee'd, church'd, glad handed, insinuated, and prayed with rigour, so to rise barely three years on to the office of Bowling Club President. Promptly identified as a *Creeping Jesus*, Alan was yet seen to possess bureaucratic skills which might prove useful to a village in decay. The conveyancing arm of his business reviving as cashed-up gentrifiers willing to pay top dollar for decaying cottages *on tank water* at last began to arrive, the President found himself stepping out with Nerys Ferris. The relationship ended, loudly, less than a week after Nerys Ferris moved up and into her second house on a hill.

Sensing the absence of empathy, animals seemed not to respect Alan Goodge. Ignoring water-filled bottles scattered by the Club President, local dogs persistently defecated, en masse, upon the close-shaven bowling green. That the worst offenders seemed always to trail Ronald Borthwick led Alan Goodge repeatedly to confront the village drunk with threat to poison any and all of his dogs "should they crap on his green again." A string of additional, non-canine atrocities being seen to accompany Ronald in and around the club, the President contrived to secure the numbers for renewed banishment of the drunkard and one-time *suspected strike saboteur*. The dog pack continued to misbehave on the green. Ronald's banishment was rescinded, on the grounds of amusement trumping outrage, following the swearing in of Alan Goodge's successor.

Alan Goodge failed to regain consciousness upon falling from a bicycle under magpie assault, having neglected to don the plastic ice-cream container mandatory in springtime. The assailant, swooping from the norfolk pine dominating the former mine accountant's front yard, was a descendant of the notorious *Fritz*, he who early in the twentieth century, from the angophora located between creek and schoolyard, had conducted a forward defence of his family against schoolchildren, teacher, and forgetful passers-by. Upon meeting an accommodating partner, Fritz's great great grandson had seized the opportunity to move uphill to a more salubrious neighbourhood, and breed.

Unique in having taken out funeral insurance, Alan Goodge lies beneath pink-veined marble, lettered in silver and featuring, behind oval glass, a coloured photo of himself, smiling. A local wit has added a Hitler moustache. Stoutly Anglican, he rests on the wrong side of a disputed border, in Roman Catholic.

NADIA LUCIA VELLA

Born 11 October, 1894, Siggiewi, Malta

Departed this life 4 February, 1943

Ave Maria

In 1913, the scream of an injured miner accompanied an accident involving the assembly of empty skips near the drift mouth. The high pitch of the scream attracting more than the usual attention, the injured miner was discovered to be a woman, Nadia Vella. How long a woman had been working in the pit, not least a woman of Maltese extraction, was never determined. Management dispensed with her services.

Decline of the British Empire having darkened Malta's economic future, the island government encouraged emigration. Nadia and husband Joseph duly stowed away and by nefarious means avoided the restrictions of White Australia. Following an inter-island pathway already well-trodden in response to reported shortages of labour on antipodean coalfields, The Maltese diaspora occupied tents on the pit fringes, moving to other pits according to demand. Nadia never revealed at what point she began to pretend to be male.

Nadia and Joseph produced a son, Peter Paul, before financial pressures motivated Joseph's travel to the goldfields of Western Australia, where he vanished without trace, and without remittance, after less than a year. Peter Paul was with Nadia's assistance able to fudge the figures and enter the pit well before attaining the legal working age of fourteen. A market slump saw him depart the pit for the Wondabyne quarry, south of Gosford, and remain there, happily more or less above ground. Nadia after persistent application was taken on by a cake shop in Gateshead, dispensing pies and sausage rolls, cream buns, vanilla slices, jam doughnuts, neenish tarts and the like, wielding mock cream and tomato sauce with alacrity, until her untimely occlusion behind the counter. Colourful amongst her modest estate was a collection of tourist brochures, in mint condition, the dream of a holiday in Malta proving in the end unaffordable on a cake shop counter attendant's wage.

It was Nadia's misfortune to require cemetery space while Ronald Borthwick was on active service, if loosely, and briefly, against the Japanese, and Jimmy Treloar installed as gravedigging temp. Bereaved Vellas found it necessary themselves to complete the excavation for Nadia's interment, during which time the deceased lay at rest in the front room for longer than was usual. The family were also required to fill the grave. Treloar being a *suspected strike saboteur*, with whom the Vellas also had personal issues concerning a niece, vindictive malfeasance was suspected. Jimmy claimed to have mislaid Nadia's booking.

Nadia's grave features a modest ornamental cross embedded with miniature icon, a reproduction of a seventeenth-century Spanish 'Virgin With Child.' Fashioned by monumental mason, Vincent 'Jumpy' Bates, the memorial evinces a budget conscious Catholicism.

BRADLEY STEVEN OSMAN
12 April 1955 – 1 June 2017

Brad Osman played hooker for Penrith in the days when scrums were still a contest, and was a keen if lumbering surfer. His grandfather had fought on the victor's side at Gallipoli. His mother spread vegemite on turkish toast. Early into a pilgrimage to the *Surf Mecca* that in November 1968 was Noosa Heads, he had swung the Impala into an overgrown hole in roadside bush, gateway to a hidden track rippling with corrugations which murdered suspensions and thus helped keep secret a mysterious surfing spot known as The Pit. On an overcast blustery morning, spinifex on the dunes bent double, silvery undersides of banksia exposed, The Pit seemed a ghost town. Dark and cold. A set from a black and white movie where residents peered from behind curtains and visitors disappeared without trace. The surf was also dark. Thick and all over the place. Brad and mates did not enter the water. The pub was deserted except for a fat drunk who barked and a skinny glassie with one arm in a sling, before a shift from a nearby pit traipsed in, filthy and staring. Brad and mates quietly vacated the premises. Brad went on to become one of few league players from the Penrith district of the time to have prospects beyond the ruination of his knees, thanks to a biggish win on Keno. A mouthy halfback recommended Brad invest his winnings in property.

Secret waves with country soul, viewed through the Impala's tinted windows, lingered long in Brad's head as city surf became choked. Beaten for waves by foul-mouthed grommets, he found time to reflect.

Everyone he knew, everyone he met waiting for a wave, or over a steak sandwich in a beer garden, everyone of an age, he observed, exhibited a similar tendency to reflect on past times. Good times. Chugging up and down the coast in old cars. Dirt roads. Boiling radiators. Deep fried food. Drinking, underage and burnt, in a public bar. Cops cruising past. Girls in terry-towelling jumpsuits with zip-up fronts. Secret waves with country soul. Don't get me started, they all said.

With his purchase of a creaking hotel frequented by a shrinking clientele of coal miners, Brad Osman realised the mature wave hunter's dream. The local mine was not long for this world. If global economics didn't kill King Coal, the Greenies would. The Pit was sitting pretty, in real estate terms, to *take off*. Brad determined to achieve a balance between raising the tone of his premises and preserving character. Four-wheel drives with child-restraint capsules were soon turning off the expressway to admire the feature wall of antique tools and black and white photos of gaunt men staring into the lens, enjoy the family beer garden, formerly the recreational pasture of pit ponies on their Sundays off. As well as day trippers, Brad also hoped to secure a host of brand-new *regulars* – regulars who would behave themselves – sourced from the housing development set to carpet the headland when it obtained the legal go ahead. Ronald Borthwick promptly left no stone unturned in furnishing Brad ample excuse to re-ban the one-time gravedigger from the establishment. The April Fools Eve shotgun was the last straw. The village drunk claimed he had been betrayed.

Bradley's headstone resembles the top half of a Malibu surfboard, positioned with lack of craft in friable, sandy loam, and vulnerable in summer to an average southerly buster.

VINCENT DESMOND BATES
7 May 1907 – 25 July 1975
Husband of Mary (Molly)
Father of Gregory, Alice, and Grace
RIP Jumpy

Vincent's nickname – 'Jumpy' – derives from his being so concentrated upon a piece of stone as to be unaware of person or persons entering his workshop, whereupon, discerning a presence, the mason would give a noticeable start.

The earliest grave in The Pit cemetery, a crypt housing stillborn Mary O'Donnell, parents James and Janet, dating from the early nineteenth century, is acknowledged to be the work of Tristram Connor, he formerly of Speke, south of Liverpool, Lancashire, England. Detected supplementing masonic income with petty theft and poaching, Connor found himself transported for seven years. Gaining his ticket of leave and changing his name to Bates, he ventured north to establish masonic credentials in the Newcastle hinterland. That coal mining was dangerous, the region short of doctors, did no harm to professional prospects. Tristram Connor married his quarryman's daughter. The couple produced an apprentice, George, who in time produced apprentice Desmond, who produced apprentice Vincent 'Jumpy' Bates. Much of the older stone dotting The Pit cemetery evidences the registered mark of Bates Masonry, a crossed hammer and chisel, perhaps, it is theorised, a sly wink to leftist politics, or a dig at freemasonry, or both.

Jumpy hewed stone within a cloud of stone dust, surrounded by stone, implements with which to work stone, stone works-in-progress and stone failures, in a distressed tin shed located at the rear of the Bates cottage. A hefty wooden bench at the sole window sagged under antique stonework reference manuals. The origin of the weighty tomes – stained and yellowing, crowded in illustration of crosses and christs on crosses, virgins mary, angels, urns, columns, obelisks, drapes, scrolls and cornices, eggs-and-darts, acorns and *fleurs de lys*, even gargoyles, seemingly dating back to the mediaeval, beautifully proportioned and specifically dimensioned for the mason's purpose – was a mystery. Transported felon Tristram Connor could not have smuggled the books abroad on his enforced sea voyage. Theft from a colonial competitor prior to departure north, with bullocky, was mooted. The profusion of illustrations reminded Jumpy of the da Vinci notebooks.

Vincent wed Mary "Molly" Cork, eldest daughter of a Broadmeadow station master, the union producing three children before Mary saw fit to conclude relations. Thereafter the couple, both of the Roman faith, commenced independent cohabitation, she indoors, he out, at increasing distance. After a decent interval, Jumpy took to frequenting The Pit, the cemetery of which featured some of his best work, while the pub featured talk of an unnamed female companion, also Romanised, resident in the vicinity of Nord's Wharf, on the lake.

The dust which took Vincent Bates was not of the same composition as that which took several of his neighbours, but the end result was identical.

Vincent is commemorated by a pointed neo-Gothic headstone, trefoil at the apex, bas-relief buttressed upon vertical edges, executed in pale Hawkesbury sandstone sourced from the Gosford quarry worked by friend Peter Paul Vella. Crafted by Jumpy himself in anticipation, a tourist brochure featuring images of graves in the Santa Maria Addolorata Cemetery, Paola, Malta, was consulted as reference, the brochure, also provided by Peter Paul, having been an inclusion in his mother's legacy.

Today, Noel Bates and offspring continue the family tradition within several glass and chrome fronted premises, servicing several cemeteries, in several towns, offering memorials tending to the over-seas-produced generic, in addition to a range of other funereal and commemorative products and services.

NON-DENOMINATIONAL/
OTHER

UNA LEAH GEMMELL
2.12.1876 – 21.8.1943
Everlasting Uncertainty

THOMAS GORDON GEMMELL
9.4.1878 – 24.9.1946
Gorgie Forever

There is no dedicated Communist Section in the cemetery. Had such been the case, had the municipal council not been dominated by coal management, later by real estate agents and property developers, the Red Sector would have dwarfed all religious sectors combined. Una Gemmell was heard frequently to remark that had Lenin known just how many party members had been buried from bourgeois convenience under the auspices of opiates of the people, the then leader of the communist world would have suffered major infarction long before his recorded series of strokes.

Gemmells Una, Thomas, Leonard and Hugh rest in identical geometric concrete tombs resonant, some have said, of Soviet bloc architecture. A heavy, rectilinear block, resolutely inscribed, squats upon one end of an even heavier rectilinear slab, the mass of concrete physically and psychologically seeming to assert that the resident below, even had they wanted, could never leave. Laid out in formal grid, the Gemmell ossuary is further remarked to present as an exemplar of centrally planned housing for the dead. Black sheep children Alec and Amy, grandson Andrew, grew to embrace less severe eternities, elsewhere.

Una Gemmell, née Mackie, would have liked to have been born Rosa Luxemburg, the revolutionary heroine's summary execution and hurling into a Berlin canal by members of the Freikorps during the Spartacist uprising of 1919 excepted. Even that fate might have been borne by the Gemmell matriarch had it led to the triumph of revolutionary socialism. Emigration reflected Una's conclusion that socialism's prospects were improved in the new land. Finding women in Australia not permitted further underground than six feet, Una overpowered dismay through electing herself a sometime Commissar of The Pit, a one-woman above-ground *blocking unit*, driving troops forward, under fire, to industrial victory and the inevitable triumph of the proletariat. Her wire-framed spectacles possessed the ability to focus interrogation into a single scorching beam, leaving the interrogated feeling small, and charred in the chest.

Despite commitment to *levelling* and *solidarity*, Una was not above insular rivalry, notably with Cora Dell 'Ma' Mayfield, a forty-year contest for which Una could always cite unarguable political justification: Ma Mayfield was a *moderate*. Solid, but a *moderate*. That solid moderation in a coal community was well to the left of solid moderation elsewhere cut no ice with Una Gemmell. A matriarchal competition in production of sons concerned not so much the desire to boast a superior quantity of progeny labouring underground, although on occasion such boasting had been heard, but rather the ability to sway voting in Lodge meetings and so determine policy and action. Disinterested parties, given the chance to speak, would at times belabour the point that The Pit was situated in the northern coalfields, where immigrants of protestant persuasion predominated. Comparison with the southern fields, where catholic arrivals and Romanised pits held sway, rendered local procreative output insubstantial.

The news of son Alec's late conversion to Catholicism shifted the ground alarmingly beneath his mother. Una was aware her middle son was different, but this was taking things to extremes.

Matriarchal feuding rippled through pit, pub, church and co-op until Una's decease, of tuberculosis. Even after, ripples were still felt as Ma Mayfield tried unsuccessfully not to speak ill of the dead.

Una Gemmell died disappointed. Fascism, clearly backpedalling west from Stalingrad, was nevertheless at Una's time of dying not utterly ground into the dirt from whence it had arisen and consigned forever to the dustbin of history, the long march to Berlin having proven for its most ardent fellow traveller a massed offensive too far. Ronald Borthwick situated Una in the corner of Non-Denominational/Other farthest from Ma Mayfield's reserved place of rest, in the farthest corner of Methodist. The prospect of argumentative female spirits wandering at night troubled the drinking gravedigger. In the event, the Mayfield family moved to Kellyville, west of Sydney, to take advantage of a labour shortage in suburban road building, and burial elsewhere.

Thomas 'Gordy' Gemmell found bricklaying – his father's line of work – lacking in appeal. Considered equally unappealing were the other places of employ for the undereducated in Edinburgh's Gorgie district: the production line at McVitie and Price Biscuits; or the liquefication of bones, hoofs and other animal products in the reduction arm of Cox's Glue and Gelatine Works. Football seemed to offer a way out. Gordon was nippy and could cross a good ball.

Trialling for Heart Of Midlothian, fast but shortish Gordy was found too easy for big men to knock over. Tynecastle Park bid him quick goodbye. The following weekend, still out of sorts, Gordy punched a Celtic supporter whose sister Una, upon detaching Gordy from her sibling, liked what she saw, and became pregnant in haste. Gordon's move west to the *dear green place* on the Clyde was less hasty, but never in doubt. Labour in the Blantyre pit alongside the in-laws, the rapid-fire production of three sons in a small tenement, the unstable mood of clan patriarch 'Wild' Bill Mackie, tested the union of Edinburgh and Glasgow. The blood of Glasgow appeared to win out in son Hugh, that of Edinburgh to make inroads with Alec, the youngest, Leonard, to be caught somewhere midstream.

Then there was politics. Where Gordon saw industrial struggle, unionism, Mackies *en masse* saw the broader political canvas of revolutionary socialism. That the Edinburgh interloper spoke of fairness, right and wrong, rather than objective historical inevitability, saw the footballing failure tagged a *bourgeois moralist* at the meal table. Gordon considered eating elsewhere but such prospects were slim. Relief was to descend in an epiphany granted to Una, also at the meal table: clan Mackie, Lanarkshire's sodden greyness, and Scottish revolutionary prospects were equally dismal, and emigration, as soon as could be arranged, historically inevitable.

Free of in-laws, granting zeal and inevitability to Una and eldest son Hugh, staunch unionism saw Gordon active in the 1909 'Peter Bowling strike'; agitate against conscription in 1916/17; trampled by a police horse at Rothbury in 1929; march to Greta Cemetery for the burial of Norman Brown, killed by a police bullet; admit, in the 1930s, when the Lockout wage cuts were restored, that communists *did get things done*; emerge victorious from the record-breaking 1941 Stay-In, and thereafter welcome retirement on the newly legislated miners' pension. Gordon's Bolshevik better half came to embrace him, intermittently, as that rare thing, *a good husband and father*, albeit *politically naïve*.

For a single winter in 1935, Gordon also discovered footballing balm in mentoring The Pit Under 10 Soccer Team, leading his charges undefeated to the Grand Final. Ronald Borthwick scored the winning goal, for the opposition, purposefully driving the ball into his own net, past The Pit's goalkeeper Jimmy Treloar. Coach Gordy, by his own admission, never recovered: "The worst own goal I've seen in over forty years of football." Under interrogation, Ronald Borthwick testified to noticing keeper Jimmy was distracted in picking a cat-head burr out of a bare foot and, the ball happening to be available, he, Ronald, was unable to help himself. And, he added, it was only a game.

At night, in season, mist folded up and over the rim of fringing hills, like milk up a saucepan, to slowly drown The Pit. Walking home late from watering holes was rendered a sometime bruising affair. Gordon died of injuries sustained in failing to take a sharp bend and plummeting into a rock-strewn pit subsidence.

LEONARD KEITH GEMMELL
5.11.1911 – 13.1.1975

The typical coal miner was not tall. Leonard Gemmell, even then, was short. Delayed puberty, not sprouting a whisker until seventeen, thence barely making five foot, further sapped the youngest Gemmell's confidence. Keeping up with the family's Glaswegian anger, not least the monumental ferocity of oldest brother and comparative giant Shug, was especially debilitating. The fury in Leonard's blood, it was discovered, was, unsettlingly, manifest *only in drink.* Further discovery, that he was rarely able to stop at one, at two refreshments finding himself consumed by rage, Leonard took to be an affirmation: the genetic legacy, wrath, had not wholly drained away by son number three. He was not entirely convinced this was a good thing.

Leonard and ponies, any pony, and there were many, were tight. Leonard bore tidbits. His pockets were long chewed through. Proximity to ponies, the rhythmic tracking back and forth of wheeling, was soothing. Meditative. Wheelers changed places every quarter. Ponies stayed where they were. They knew their routes. Leonard's favourite, a knowing Shetland from Breeza, wore a long fringe and answered to the name of Roy. Behind the pub, well lubricated, Leonard all but killed Hec Morgan, suspected of mistreating Roy. It was a misunderstanding.

Emerging from the Stay-In, dazzled by daylight, peer pressure recruited Leonard into a mob of taller miners hunting down *suspected strike saboteurs* Borthwick and Treloar. Dragged into thick bush, the blacklegs were stripped naked and hurled into a shallow, coal-fouled swamp. The spongey muck, cold beneath the surface, was alarming for what it might contain. Attempts to rise were discouraged with sharpened bamboo spears. Fred Platt deployed a bullwhip. Leonard's discomfort at the boys' sentence was washed away in the pub.

A casualty of 1958 and unskilled except for a way with ponies, Leonard had a rare happy thought: he would find work as a stablehand. Equine job-seeking as far abroad as Scone without success, it seemed to Leonard that *his class* always barred the way to stable work. Pit ponies were not the same as horses. Resigned, he entrained on the cheap to the Illawarra coalfields, slept rough, and tramped the coastal coal pit road – Helensburgh, Coalcliff, Clifton, Corrimal, Bulli, Russell Vale, Mt Kembla – without finding work. Returning to The Pit, he found wife Jeannie gone, inland, with a postal worker from Charmhaven.

Leonard never remarried. There was, it was said, a later woman in his life, a housewife residing in a coastal village south of Newcastle, unhappily wed to an agent for a life insurance company who on occasion overnighted in far flung towns, during which time Leonard and the nameless unhappy housewife pursued liaison. Further talk, under the influence, progressively projected the husband dead, killed in the war; or having survived, run down by the Cardiff RSL courtesy bus; or king hit from behind by a rival insurance agent outside the Boatrowers Hotel, Stockton; or, finally arriving at the narrative considered most likely, throttled and dumped in an abandoned pit working by a lover – no names, no pack drill – acting under instruction from the victim's wife. Leonard, unsmiling, neither confirmed nor denied, even in his cups.

He died beach fishing at a village south of Newcastle. The salmon were running. Brother Alec, cavilled out in 1956 and long gone to the refuge of Kings Cross, was unable to be located for the lowering.

After filling Leonard's grave, Ronald Borthwick progressed to the pub to top up and remember, rowdily, as he was increasingly wont to do: "Flat on my back in the black swamp. Are you with me? Slimy little bastard, brown with yellow stripes. In the armpit. Big red and black bastard next, down south. In the groin, it was. Another one, maybe more, up my crack. Then the bastards were all over everywhere. Leeches' picnic, it was. Ha! Ha! Leeches union picnic. Ha! Ha! Ask Skinny. He knows all about it. All about it. Leonard didn't look keen. Give him that. Give him that. Rest in peace, Leonard. Fred Platt was keen. Fred had his bullwhip. I buried Fred too. Are you with me?"

Interest in the broadcast was scant. Backs were turned, the verandah visited. Ronald had by this time buried almost all who had participated in the events recalled. Straggler Fizzer Phillips, alone in Retired Miners Corner, slept through the remembrance.

HUGH ALEXANDER GEMMELL
4.5.1908 – 1.4.1985
Read the Russians

In the aftermath of Sunday bathing, brushing, and candle-waxing, head disproportionately large in relation to his body, and mostly forehead, Hugh 'Shug' Gemmell bore a distinct resemblance to Lenin. The likeness, deliberate, lay concealed beneath a coating of coal during the working week.

Historical grievance illuminated by alcohol rendered Shug Gemmell amiably violent, tending less amiable with passage of time. Upon emigrating, Shug had soon concluded that historical grievance, sectarian contest, tribal feud, lacked pungency in the New World. Yes, the ancient antagonisms had been transported, but the rebellious blood appeared to thin, the old aggravations to seep from the skin, and evaporate in antipodean sunshine. That miners went to the beach on a day off said all that needed to be said, averred Shug, proceeding to say much more, mainly on the shining light of the Soviet State, flavoured by mature breath of whiskey and milk, tobacco, The Pit, something far more foul from Mrs Gemmell's stove. At the heart of the gastric ire, still and always, lay Lanarkshire, blackened and brooding, the *blood hardness* defiant in spite of escape, in spite of hating the ancient *hame*, as any number of Gemmells always had hated it, not least since Blantyre, the Dixons pits, wherein Matthew, thirty one, John, twenty two, William Gemmell, nineteen, alongside Peter Mackie, thirty one, had perished with two hundred and three other men and boys in the disaster of 1877.

At fifteen, Shug attended 'Red Reg' Worsley's classes in Marxism, where he excelled. Enlightenment was promptly shaded by the con-tradictions of mechanisation in the pit. The German mentor had declared mechanisation an inevitable step on the road to socialism. With due respect to the German mentor, the Federation argued that, local capacity exceeding demand, mechanisation was unnecessary, raised unemployment and safety concerns, and was to be stridently opposed by industrial action.

The unquiet relationship between *theory* and *practice*, the "fooking dialectic!", was to trouble Shug a lifetime. Lenin's NEP. Stalin's Show Trials. The Nazi-Soviet Pact. Hitler two hundred miles inside the Ukraine and motoring. The Polish Officers. Kruschev's *Secret Speech*. Hungary. Czechoslovakia. Mao. The peripatetic party line. The contor-tions required. Shug contorted more than most. Inwardly he churned. Angry, hewing to the line, he became angrier. He smote errant trapper boys like flies. Ronald Borthwick was slow to develop the necessary radar. Shug Gemmell was the first adult to refer to Ronald Borthwick as "You fat little shite!" Ronald was shortish and squat, but not yet, at fourteen, on his first day underground, fat. Additional commentary followed: "Never troost a fooking redhead!" The relationship attained maturity amid the 1941 Stay-In. Shug's one-handed suspension by the neck of Jimmy Treloar, the suspected strike saboteur's chalky-boned legs dancing the hangman's jig over scattered brown bottles, the Scot's free hand a raised fist resembling a blackened cauliflower, spurred Ronald to speak. Jimmy, it was reported, folded to the pit floor like a rag doll. Ronald was spared Gemmell violence by the arrival of Lodge President Dickie Jones.

In the throes of retirement, Shug's antique politik became entertain-ment for the young. Encouraged to rant, the rickety, frame-pushing commo would flay *capitalists, fellow travellers,* any and all *enemies of the people,* showering spittle and rolling his "R's" way beyond Scottish quotidian. The keeping of a straight face by his provocateurs was seen as a test. By the time Shug was detailing how *the rruling class* used *morrtgages* to render the working class as *docile as ffoooooking donkeys,* the disrespectful young could usually contain their mirth no longer and Shug would realise he had, again, been had.

A heart attack as would fell a Clydesdale took Shug *across the white bridge.* Occurring deep in the night, the cardiac event was catalysed by a shotgun blast within the nearby cemetery. Shug did not live to hear the second shotgun blast, shortly after.

In Loving Memory Of
JOE KEATS
23 February 1895 – 12 March 1950

As far as can be discerned from exhaustive study of the published *oeuvre*, Karl Marx never saw fit to pronounce on the game of cricket. A rare ideological *lacuna*, the absence came as profound relief to Joe Keats, stalwart of the Militant Minority Movement, believer in the inevitable progress of historical materialism, and lover of the game. The Mentor, Joe suspected, had he turned his considerable intellect to the subject, might well have disapproved of the activity on numerous grounds, all of which Joe had elected to ignore when it came to donning the flannels. For Joe had discovered early on that batting *calmed the fevered political min*d. At bat, all he thought about was the ball. And to which part of the field he might despatch it. Fielding likewise soothed, unless assigned to the outfield against weak opposition whence, the ball rarely visiting, the mind became prey to dialectical conjecture. Joe preferred to field in the slips. There was no time for political thought in the slips.

The 1932-33 England-Australia "Bodyline" series was to cause Joe particular perturbance. English fast bowlers Larwood and Voce were both coalminers and sons of coalminers. Bradman was bourgeois. There were long dark nights of ideological brawl with Moscow-aligned Shug Gemmell, the elastic inconclusiveness of which was no doubt nourished by both Lenin and Stalin echoing The Mentor in neglecting to offer a view on the game.

Larwood and Voce had been rescued from the Nottinghamshire pits by professional cricket. No such escape was ever to present itself to Joe. That son Cedric evinced total disinterest in the game was possibly more of a disappointment than the offspring's drift to Trotskyism and beyond.

Off season, uninterested in football, Joe would attempt to ease a troubled mind by contributing articles of impeccably impenetrable revolutionary logic to *Red Leader,* organ of the MMM, and the Miners Federation newspaper *Common Cause.* Most if not all of his submissions were deemed too prolix for publication, let alone digestion.

Joe went on to recruit and captain the only recorded all-communist cricket team ever to play the game. The Red XI enjoyed a single season in a northern coalfields district competition, losing every game before disbanding. Love of the game saw Joe continue to play alongside reformists and other moderates, whilst drawing the line at teaming with management.

Joe Keats died in 1950, of lockjaw, having slashed a foot on ancient corrugated iron, the remnants of a pioneer miner's shanty unearthed while planting silver beet in the back garden.

He lies in the sandy soil of Non-Denominational/Other, his allocation, E23, colonised by red-tipped pigface, dandelion, and sparse clumps of mongrel grass. Dunes, advancing inland, swallowing cemetery fence and easternmost graves, edge towards E23. The long-term viability of the Non Denominational/Other sector is considered threatened.

Dedicated To The Memory Of

CEDRIC MAYFIELD-KEATS

18 May 1924 – 7 July 2001

On The Road Again

Sexually and politically precocious, Cedric Mayfield-Keats's boyhood is remembered as nothing if not outstanding. Relentlessly disruptive in class, the relentless thrashing which followed seemed only to stimulate Cedric to more virulent infraction. Cedric somehow knew the delivery dates of Department of Education canes – bi-annually, in packs of six – and intercepting them would doctor the ends with drawing pins, causing the instruments to split after one or two strokes. Cedric was also known to rub coloured chalk on his hands so that when it came his turn, his hand appeared to explode. He possessed the ability to fart at will. With directional control. By lifting a cheek and blasting away at an angle, it was said, he could aim farts. This capacity, claimed Cedric, in enclosed settings rendered wind a political weapon.

Sexual precocity led Cedric to exhibit a pre-pubertal knack in relations behind slack heaps, in backyard chicken coops and aviaries. Nerys Ferris was unique in being never of interest, greatly aggrieving the young Queen Of The Pit. At ten, Cedric introduced Karen Vella, eleven, to smoking and kissing. A finely-tuned capacity to divert blame saw Jimmy Treloar fingered as the guilty party and merit undying Vella family wrath. Dot Borthwick's interest in Cedric persisted beyond chicken coops and puberty, to peak in a tenacious stalking episode in Balmain, Sydney, where Cedric had found work on the docks after escaping The Pit and, he hoped, Dot.

Cedric embraced communism at twelve, attending meetings in Cessnock with his father, before at thirteen converting to his mother's Trotskyism. In his final year of schooling, perusing his father Joe's collection of *Common Cause*, organ of the Miners Federation, Cedric came across the following:

We as members of the Federation protest against the action of the State Education Department in respect to school children being compelled to salute the flag and sing on Monday mornings, and that the Executive be instructed to protect the parents who refuse to allow their children to go through this farce.

Inspired, Cedric's last day of school saw him galvanise the student body to assail the apogee of imperial ceremony, Empire Day. The day of insurrection culminated in Red Ced, legs spread, vomiting a rope-like line down the middle of the road, the outcome of multiple underage drinks filched from the pub verandah rail, whereupon Cedric departed The Pit and was not seen again for forty-six years.

He returned behind the wheel of a bronze Valiant AP6, tinny on roof, humpback caravan in tow. The disappointed communist, after a brief flirtation with Bakuninist anarchism, had replaced belief in the perfectibility of mankind with a love of driving, amused by the thought that, had he lived, Trotsky might have done much the same thing.

Cedric was one of three to attend the funeral of Ronald Borthwick. The unannounced return of Maria Vella, sixty, looking fifty, if that, accompanied by a middle-aged man who smoked brightly coloured cigarettes, had occasioned Ronald's end. Cedric remembers:

"Ronnie came banging on the caravan door. In the middle of the night. I didn't ask him in. He wouldn't fit through the door. He looked like shit in shorts. Resch's longneck in each hand. Purple. He'd turned purple by then. Speckled with frags of potato crisp. Chicken flavour. That yellow colour. I couldn't help thinking I'd never met a chicken that colour. He barked at me like one of his dogs:"

"I was thinking about Arthur Scargill when they turned up!"

"That was the first thing Ronnie said. I waited for him to go into detail."

"Dominic smokes coloured cigarettes. Me and him look like two peas in a pod, Dot reckons. Except the hair. Black as coal, his is. Same as the little girls. Back in Malta. My granddaughters. Two little girls. Hair black as coal, Maria said. Didn't take off her sunnies. Huge round ones. She asked was I married to Nerys Ferris. Was I? Was I married to Nerys Ferris? Jimmy told her me and Nerys Ferris were engaged. At the Bellevue, this was. The Bellevue. So Maria was wasting her time. Then he jumped her. Mongrel. Jumped her. At the Bellevue, this was. So she broke his wrist and took off. Me fetching beer was his idea. Bastard always had a plan. Now he tells her I'm dead. Her and Dominic. When they drove in. Told them I'm dead. Liver conked out. The grog. Ashes got thrown somewhere. Scotland maybe. Where we come from. No grave. Maria and Dominic might as well fly straight back to Malta. Bastard always had a plan. I'm not dead. They saw me. Dot made tea. They left early so they didn't miss their flight. I watched the flashing red light fly over the cemetery."

"Then he ploughed off back into the night. Next thing I knew Ronnie was dead. So was Jimmy."

Cedric designed and assembled the materials for his own grave. A low, concrete edifice bordered in liverish brick, checkerboard head-stone in cream and white brick, edged in assorted bathroom and kitchen tiles, the materials cadged from several demolition sites,

Cedric's name and dates are engraved on a Valiant hubcap above a red reflector in the shape of a naked woman. Assembly of the memorial, to strict specification, was undertaken by a retired builder from Lake Macquarie who did odd jobs and was willing to travel. The memorial does not conform to cemetery trust regulations but remains to date undisturbed by authority. It is theorised that money may have changed hands.

CORAL PATRICIA MAYFIELD
5 February 1903 – 20 May 1987
Mother of Cedric, Margaret, Colin and Russell

Coral at seventeen was disowned by her parents for unconscionable promiscuity in the guise of revolutionary politics. In the afterglow of Soviet success rushing to cohabit with *rampant commo* Joe Keats, giving birth to another leftist firebrand in son Cedric, the couple developed irreconcilable differences over Lenin's New Economic Policy and separated with Stalin's ascent to leadership of The Party. Coral moved on and in with a follower of the increasingly out-of-favour Trotsky, one Freddie Billings, of Wallsend, to whom Coral presented three children. Freddie, in the end, saw his political mission as more important than the successful rearing of young.

Moving on again, Coral and the Billings children settled in a timber hut on a flood-prone dairy farm near Raymond Terrace, where Coral, under the tutelage of farmer's son Terry, quickly learned to milk and otherwise tend to dairy cattle while her children attempted schooling when not engaged in farm labour, the slave-like intensity of which, in according precisely with their mother's political explications, discouraged young thoughts of pursuing a life on the land. Further discouraged from venturing anywhere near coal, or marrying anyone who did, the offspring relocated to city suburbs and labour in car yards, furniture warehousing, and hospitals.

Children dispersed, Coral moved in with farm widow Enid and son Terry. Enid saw fit to convince herself that Terry and Coral were not engaged in an unmarried physical relationship whilst approving Coral's adroitness in farm management, not least after the floods of 1955 and 1971. Despite political leanings, Coral knew how to work banks and bankers. For a time she also managed accommodation with Terry's espousal of agrarian socialism when times were bad, rampant capitalism when good.

Coral returned to The Pit in 1975, by default inheriting the Mayfield cottage, her siblings dead or departed and disinterested. Joining the Progress Association, the mature firebrand fought against the establishment of a housing estate on a large parcel of real estate purchased from Anglican and Catholic churches and the mining company which, in selling miners their houses but not the land upon which they stood, enabled demolition upon decease of the owner. Protest saw the proposed estate appear to diminish in size and not steal all of the best views, on paper, but not go away. Closure of the pit heightened the threat.

Early in April 1985, en route to inspect a burial plot with a view to purchase, it was Coral's misfortune to come across the bodies of Jimmy Treloar and Ronald Borthwick, dead of shotgun wounds.

Coral not long after sold the cottage to newcomer Nerida Humphries and moved to a nursing home managed by the catholic church, close to Wyong railway station, making it easier for her children and families to visit. Cedric proved her most attentive offspring. Coral did not participate in the rosary or communion, but was known to enjoy the singing of hymns. She and Faith Phillips, sister of 'Fizzer', for a time resident in the same nursing home, did not appear to recognise each other.

Coral's grave features a traditional round-top headstone in recycled marble derived from a late Victorian kitchen benchtop, white, grey-streaked, in colour, of size sufficient to furnish a second memo-rial upon the death of the stonemason's wife. The mason, Gregory Bates, son of Vincent 'Jumpy' Bates, was to become the last of the *hands-on* Bates stonemasons, the family firm under economic pres-sure turning to outsourcing, to foreign lands, for memorials. Gregory would also turn out to be the last in the Bates line familiar with the term *mates rates.*

NERIDA LOUISE HUMPHRIES
12.11.1933 – 2.7.2010
Peace

Nerida Humphries' husband, suburban accountant, left after twenty years of marriage to move to an adjoining suburb with his reception-ist of one year. Nerida experienced relief as she had been wrestling with the question of how to tell Robert she was leaving him with-out hurting his feelings. She also thought, in respect of his secre-tary, be careful what you wish for, Robert. In the event, she departed mediation with sufficient to purchase a new Volkswagen kombi, a second-hand potting wheel and furnace, and a run-down miners' cot-tage in a dying village.

Nerida had dabbled in clay pottery while on marital duty, the latter including the raising of three less than gifted, egotistical children. Freed, discovering to her delight that her creativity would not be con-strained by potting orthodoxy, she stumbled into the realm of what she termed *organic sculptural pottery*, and there set up shop. Her pots, if that was what they were, ballooned in size, colour, and organic com-plexity, and, the artist would freely admit, uselessness. But they looked interesting. Almost *alive*, some said.

In 1986, a late-coming resident, newly subscribed to The Pit Progress Association and keen to demonstrate commitment, Nerida proposed that The Association seek heritage classification for The Pit as *an historic mining village*. Seconded by another recent arrival, Herbert Hobbs, the motion – voted down overwhelmingly by longer term members – had within twenty-four hours given a decided fillip to decidedly *unhistoric* home improvements.

The four-room cottages, remaining largely original and decaying at heart, overnight began to outwardly sport thickly personalised makeup, whereby nineteenth-century timber verandah posts were replaced by modest Grecian columns in concrete (Neville Jones), tubular steel posts (Washery Foreman Don Frost), box-sections (Police Sergeant Mick Worsley, transferred; of late, daughter Tracey), lightweight open-web joists (Dougie Platt), some featuring curling metal ivy (Moaning Janice Jones) and Moorish-influenced ferro-cement arching (Bowling Club President Allen Goodge). Porticos shaded aluminium fascia, mock brick sheeting, cement stucco, plasterboard, 'crazy paving' with the temerity to scale walls, enlarged sliding windows, and slimline screen doors which corroded white in the salt air. Rich cream, milky lime, dark chocolate trim were the dominant colours by virtue of a Massive Once In A Lifetime Stocktake Sale at Swansea Hardware.

Housefront symmetry became popular, creating a line of rectilinear faces with aluminium-rimmed eyes above flyscreened noses and mouths, the congruity offset by ten-metre television aerials tucked jauntily behind one ear. A late trend – repositioning the aerial at the midpoint of the roof ridge to attain absolute symmetry and look neater – unjaunty – was initiated by Nerys Ferris.

Original timber was, if not routed, now in rapid retreat. Wayne Thorpe had secreted his entire timber cottage, including the verandah, within a box of cream aluminium cladding, sealed under a pyramidal blue and white terracotta tiled lid. Two slit windows faced the road with apparent deep suspicion. Thorpes embraced darkness as though in fond remembrance of the gloom of Derby, left behind generations before. Within his aluminium shell, Wayne was systematically removing all trace of organic material for deployment as winter fuel.

Alone, Nerida bucked the trend to modernity, stripping the former home of Coral Mayfield of any feature deemed *inauthentic*. Nerida's best endeavours at authenticity resulted in the house appearing more fraudulent by the day.

Nerida persistently denied involvement in a long-running affair with Herbert Hobbs, let alone to exploring a 1970s style retro threesome with Herbert and white-calico-clad wife Denise. Retired Miners Corner voted Nerida *the type*.

It was true she had belatedly loosened up, 1970s style, upon taking up residence in The Pit. Nerida's 1970s continued well into the new millennium.

A number of male visitors, said to be fellow potters and sculptors, were seen to overstay and attend to heritage restoration in and around the Humphries cottage. It was said the aroma of illegal substance could be detected in the surrounding atmosphere. Others put this down to a particularly odoriferous Indonesian cigarette in vogue within artistic and counter cultural circles.

Diagnosed late, given twelve to eighteen months, Nerida devoted her remaining time in this dimension to the creation of her own memorial headstone. The design process proved a tortuous journey. Recent regulatory restrictions governing the size, shape and symbolic nature of memorials necessitated several major changes in creative direction. Erotic forms sourced from Indian temple reliefs were deemed unsuitable.

The wording on headstones had also become subject to regulation. Nerida had at one stage opted for a notably ribald passage from Rabelais on the subject of bodily functions as a summation of life, in the hope her commemoration might surprise those who thought her straight-laced. Especially her children. Should they visit. Which she doubted. The scatalogical epitaph was to feature in parti-coloured ceramic lettering on an outsized marker shaped like a Norse runestone. Or gargantuan kipfler potato, with crude inscription, depending on point of view. Before rejection by the cemetery trust, Nerida had despatched photographs of the Rabelaisian Runestone to her children to whet their appetites for visiting.

The completed memorial, in situ, while not widely considered a work of beauty, is demonstrably an object of intrigue. Locals instruct tourists not to miss *the thing*. More than one visitor has been overheard to ask, "What on earth was she thinking?" *The thing* is compliant with current regulations.

Her children sold the cottage, as a weekender, to a middle-aged café owner and jetski rider from Sydney, for considerably more than their mother paid for it.

TIM GOODING

www.ingramcontent.com/pod-product-compliance
Lightning Source LLC
Chambersburg PA
CBHW031240260626
47169CB00007B/2391